LEASHED

HUMAN PET SHOP

LOKI RENARD

Copyright © 2023 by Loki Renard

Cover by The Book Brander

All rights reserved.

No part of this book may be reproduced in any form or by any electronic or mechanical means, including information storage and retrieval systems, without written permission from the author, except for the use of brief quotations in a book review.

1

Arkan

Ding-a-ling-a-ling!

The little bell at the door of the human pet shop rings inside my mind. I hear the creaking of the hinges, and then a great deal of psychic cursing and physical scuffling as some previous customers attempt to make a return. The psychic sound of the doorbell and the hushed telepathic whispers of a good family man trying to handle a wild human is quickly overridden by the sound of that human female's voice.

"Let me go, assholes! I'll bite your whole goddamn family!"

A smile crosses my face, a broad and excited expression that I must immediately school into composure.

She's back.

My brother sold her, assuming she was stock like any other. He did not know I had any attachment to the human woman who, by the psychic grunts of pain and calls for help is unloading every bit of her small human female fury on the unsuspecting and undeserving family who bought her. They thought she was cute. She is. They thought she would make a good family pet. They were wrong.

I emerge from the back of the shop where I was feeding a freshly caught male, to discover a young human female named Jennifer making a huge scene both in my shop and out on the street at the same time. Quite an impressive feat for a relatively small creature.

Her hands and arms are wrapped around the door frame. Her head is stuck out into the street, and her owner has her by the legs and is trying to pull her off the door and into the shop, which is going to end badly for the human if they are not more careful. They have dressed her in a style which I can only describe as a sweet little ballerina. She has a tutu on and a pink legging bodysuit to match. The rear of it snugs extra tight over her shapely human haunches, which have always been in dire need of spanking, and are even more so now.

Her owners are a couple of well-dressed Euphorians, both with cascading raven hair and highly polished scales. The woman stands back, keeping her distance with an air of haughty disapproval on her face. She is beautiful, as are all women and men of our species. She is wearing a casual floor-length gown spun in skeins of highly reflective glittering fabric, as is the fashion. Her hair has been swept into a coiled updo and is adorned with a pin denoting her as a descendent of one of the original families of Euphoria. There is an expression of pure disgust on her elegant face as she is forced to confront a display of pure animal rebellion in the human.

The man, such as he is, is also dark haired. I do believe that these two are lesser members of the Wrathelder clan. They are a family not known for patience or kindness, and most of their wealth has come from the new construction in the central city. He has cut his hair short and chooses to wear silver tips on his lower mandibular tusks. His clothing is not as formal as his wife's. He has chosen a cross between a pretense at warrior attire, with a hint of construction. His clothing is made of fake animal skin tailored to fit him perfectly, beige trousers, high brown boots, and a jerkin with mesh sewn into the fabric in various places to create an appearance of flesh and metal meeting. Together they make an absolutely disparate sight. There is nothing coherent about this little family.

He wanted to play beast master, I think. His wife probably wanted a pet for the children. The children, it seems, wanted a ballerina. My brother may have sold him a beast, but it takes more than money or privilege to tame one, and as for the other roles, this particular human was never going to be suited to any of them.

This unfortunate pet's owners are silently screaming at her to comply and obey, but the human has no telepathic powers. We Euphorians are a hyper-intelligent, advanced race of aliens who by all accounts have put aside the many petty tribulations of most civilizations. We know no war and little conflict. We are also very tall, and relative to humans, incredibly strong. It is quite remarkable then, that this one young human female in her mid-twenties is managing to best an entire family of our species.

It might help if they remembered any of the human language commands they are supposed to use when interacting with their human pet, but like many families who buy a cute human without thinking about all the responsibilities and work that comes with forging a true bond with an intelligent creature from another world, they have clearly not followed a single shred of the Human Pet Book, sold at the front and back of our store for a very reasonable 3.99.

"No! You stupid fish-scaled psychopaths! I'm not going back to that fucking store!" The human continues to protest at the top of her lungs. Of course, her owners have absolutely no idea what she is saying. To them, it is nothing but incoherent yelling, and judging by the way the lady of the house is covering her ears with her hands, it is quite upsetting.

"Let me help you," I say to the owners in a soothing telepathic tone.

"You know better than to act this way, pet," I drawl in my deep tones. I speak perfect human, and the one currently pitching a fit at the front of my store for all the world and good society to see, recognizes it instantly. Her head turns, and she shoots me a look of pure venom with her big brown human eyes.

"This is your fault, you fucking..." She goes off on another verbal tear, even more outraged now than she was before. I knew better than to think she would start behaving herself when she heard me. This is what happens when an untamed pet is sold. Jen needed a lot more training before she was ready to go to a new home.

I come forward and take the human's feet from the owner's hands. He is yanking on her alarmingly while still not managing to break her grip. Humans are not large, or strong, but they do have simian lineage in their DNA, and when they want to hold onto something, they can hold on for dear life. Still, his artless pulling and twisting could do damage to her relatively weak tendons and ligaments. If she does let go of the frame, she also has a significant chance of slamming her head into the ground, which could kill her. Humans can be surprisingly strong for their size, but they can also be easily injured.

I am careful when I take hold of her, running my hands up the curves of her body and then moving her back out into the street in the same direction as she was gripping, making it impossible for her to hold on, before tossing her up and over my shoulder in a position I've found very stable for most humans. Sure, they can kick you in the stomach, but the easy availability of a padded rear evens that risk out.

I take one hefty kick to my gut, and follow it up with a firm but not too hard slap to both of her cheeks. She lets out a squeal of outrage but stops kicking for the moment. She is out of breath. I can hear and feel her panting over my shoulder, as she finally takes a small break in the ongoing struggle against her alien captors.

"What seems to be the problem?" I address the owners.

The male sighs audibly, indicating an almost uncontrollable level of frustration. *"She's not working out. She's destroyed three couches since we took her home last week. She's eaten the children's homework every night. My son is getting a failing grade as it is. And every time we get a visitor she attempts to attack them. The final straw was when she sent my wife to the emergency room with a nasty bite. They told us we should have her destroyed."*

The human they are talking about is oblivious to their frustrations, being far too concerned instead with her own. She is about five foot five in stature, with dark eyes, caramel tan skin, and rainbow pink hair, a popular combination ever since a similarly marked human became popular in an advertisement for insurance. She is wearing what can only be described as a rainbow tutu attached to a pink bodysuit. I sell these in my store, albeit reluctantly. I call them ballerina dresses, though they're not really dresses at all. They make most humans look cute. They make this one look absolutely adorable, in spite of the fact it is clearly an aesthetic at odds with her mood. Some of the fluffy material brushes against my nose as she squirms. I do like the fact that the bodysuit provides little protection for her deserving rear, as well as snaps in the lower region which can and in all likelihood will be used to bare her ass.

Most Euphorians are capable of maintaining basic discipline with their human pets once order is established. Humans like to know where they stand. They generally do very well once they settle into a new home and new routine. Most of the pets we have sold have done very well. But there are always exceptions, and this little human has been an exception from the moment I caught her.

The owner's complaints continue in a silent tirade. My species abandoned small mouth noises early in our development and now relies almost entirely on telepathy. We are able to be much more precise with the language of the mind than we ever were with verbal speech. This shift is credited with the unprecedented peace we now live in. Of course, small children still babble, and often are the only ones in a family capable of communicating linguistically with human pets. That is because, as in all species, the young have not lost their roots to their ancestral animal past.

"We tried introducing her to the neighbor's human, but they didn't get along, and now they fight through the fence. I don't know what a bay-sic bi-ch is, but every time this one sees theirs, she shouts it at full volume."

"Introducing humans has to be done carefully," I remind them. "You can't just put them together and expect them to get along. And training is essential, especially for a human her age. She's only in her twenties. With the right training, she will be an excellent companion for the next thirty to forty years."

"I know. We had to put our last human down when he got out on the interstellar highway. We thought a younger female would be easier."

"A common misapprehension," I commiserate. My brother, Kahn, should never have sold this girl. I had words with him about it, but he said he'd found her in the stock section. I didn't put her there, and I am almost certain she was probably trying to sneak her way out when she was sold.

This is not the time for an *I told you so*, but at the time, I did contact the family and warn them that they had been sold a pet who was not entirely trained. They insisted on keeping her, of course. They thought she was cute, and at first her antics were funny. They refused to return her, and I had no legal recourse to reclaim her. That was all of three days ago.

No matter how many times I give new human owners the spiel about human care, or how many times I revise my **Alien's Guide To Keeping People As Pets**, there is no such thing as an easy human. They may be more simple than us, smaller than us, and live relatively short lives, but they are complex, social beings.

"You do have to speak to the humans. They can't hear your thoughts." I say that out loud, demonstrating how it is done. Though they are returning this young lady, there is a significant chance they will buy another. Humans have become status symbols on Euphoria. My brother and I can barely keep up with the demand from aristocratic families.

"Speaking is so..." The lady of the house makes face of disgust. *"I don't want the children picking up the habit."*

I know Kahn would have told them about speaking to their human, and I know he would not have sold her without their enthusiastic agreement. I've seen it many times before, excited families oohing and aaahing over the human pet they just picked out, promising to love him or her forever and telling me how very experienced they were with humans, having had several before.

I would be disappointed, but unfortunately, unprepared owners and difficult pets are a common enough phenomenon in my line of business. Education is important, as is righting wrongs when they arise.

"We will always accept returns," I say. *"Let's take her back and put her safely in a cage, and we can get your refund processed."*

2

Jen

I'm stuck over the shoulder of the alien, his big palm clasped over my ass to keep me in place. He touches me with casual intimacy. He holds me like he owns me. I'd almost forgotten in just the handful of days I was with the aliens who just returned me that he was this comfortable with handling me. They were not. I've sunk my teeth into more skin and scales in the last 72 hours than I have in my entire life. I'd bite him too, but the way he's holding me makes it completely impossible.

This alien is an asshole with a savior complex. He has the nerve to think turning me into a commodity to be sold is doing me a favor. I thought I'd escape the family but they have been just competent enough to keep me contained long enough to get here. Their houses are built to their size, and reaching some of the latches and things is a challenge, especially when they tie you up every chance they get. I have chafe marks around my wrists and ankles from being bound by these stupid fucking aliens.

Arkan, the alien who has me now, is eight feet tall, offensively handsome, and I hate him. I keep squirming in the effort to escape his grip, but all that happens is his fingers palm my ass a little harder in warning.

These aliens can best be described as something between an elf and an orc with just a hint of dragon besides. Arkan has the cool, calm, superior demeanor of an elf, along with the crystalline gaze and the long, flowing purple-blue hair. He has the musculature and lower tusks of an orc, and he has the light scaling on the outside of his shoulders and arms, and probably legs of a dragon with a sort of bare-ish patch along his torso, and I suppose all the way down his stomach. I don't know what environment they evolved in, and I don't give a fuck.

I've seen more of these aliens than I ever wanted to. They don't regard me as a sentient being because I can't talk like they do inside their heads, so they have a tendency to walk around me while they're naked. I've seen some alien dong, in other words, not Arkan's, but the man of the house. He was hung like the proverbial equine.

My ass is stinging from where Arkan's stupid big alien hand made contact with my rear through the stupid pet clothes that barely cover anything. The lady of this alien family thought it would be fun to get me all kinds of outfits. She must have spent a whole lot of alien money on getting me looking just right, and then I refused to wear any of it, insufferable, insulting costumes that they were. It took them a good hour to wrestle me into the clown-colored ballerina costume I'm currently wearing. Talk about humiliation.

Arkan is carrying me away from them now, to the back of the store. He tips me off his shoulder and into a human sized cage he has back there. Immediately, I see and smell that I am not alone. There's another person in a nearby cage, some guy cowering in the corner. Poor bastard. He doesn't know what's going to happen to him. He must be terrified.

"Behave yourself," Arkan warns me in perfect English.

"Go fuck yourself," I reply.

He smiles at me, flashing a big mouth full of rather sharp teeth. These aliens really look very dangerous. They're impossibly tall, and they are made like predators. But they're advanced, and so they don't use that strength aggressively, as far as I can tell. They're intellectual and they talk telepathically, and they really enjoy a very orderly world. Every part of their city is artisanal and original, including their pets, which unfortunately includes me.

"I'll deal with you later," he says. "Once I have dealt with the traumatized owners you've created."

"Fuck all of you," I respond. I'd never admit it, but I am actually very relieved to be talking to someone, because the aliens he sold me to have absolutely no idea how to communicate verbally. I've spent the last god knows how many days in a veil of tense and stressed silence.

Arkan lifts a brow at me and shakes his head in a gesture that reads very much as human. His pale, ice-colored hair falls around his powerful features in a rakish veil. Hs eyes are the color of gold and rimmed with lashes of dark blue. His chin, jaw, and entire mandibular plane is chiseled in the extreme. He's hot. He is way too fucking hot. But not too hot to hate.

I glare at him with all the loathing I can muster. This is all his fault. He did this to me. He thinks humans are animals he has the right to sell. I will make him regret ever taking me. I will ensure that every time he sells me, I ruin his reputation a little more.

I went out of my way to destroy everything at the house of the aliens where I was sold. They don't say much, but they made some very interesting noises when they discovered that I'd slashed all their furniture using what I guess was a ceremonial knife. It was hanging on the wall just begging to be used for some good old-fashioned vengeance.

After locking me away, he goes back out to the front to silently negotiate whatever it is he's going to give them in terms of compensation. I hope I'm costing him a lot more than I'm worth.

As soon as he is gone, I turn my attention to the other person in the other cage.

"Hey, buddy," I hiss.

A pair of dark eyes appears behind the bars. He's a guy, maybe in his thirties. He looks scared. He should be. There's nothing for us here on this planet. And there's no way back home that I've seen. The only small glimmer of hope I can see is that I might be able to convince this alien trader of human flesh to take me home if I am enough of a fucking pain in the ass.

"Hey," he says. "What the fuck is going on? I think I must have taken something. I'm tripping balls and seeing blue people."

"We're all tripping balls, dude. Except we're not. We've been captured by an alien who sells humans to other aliens."

"Oh fuck!" He curses and panics, wrapping his hands nervously around the bars, looking out at me with a haunted expression. He looks like an accountant or something, wearing a rumpled suit that probably looked good when he first put it on. His tie is loosened, and his shirt is open several buttons. He's wet, maybe from sweat. Maybe he fell asleep and knocked over his water bowl. Been there, done that.

"Are they going to kill us and eat us?" His first question is his deepest fear.

"Worse," I say.

He practically shits himself. "Are they going to torture us?"

"Kind of. They're going to take us into their homes and make us their pets."

His eyes widen into two saucers of concern. "What?"

"Yeah. They're going to take you into their home, like, into their family, and they're going to treat you like a fucking animal for the rest of your life."

"Do they feed us?"

"Sure."

He shifts, looking a little less concerned, which I guess makes sense. "Is it... are they nice homes?"

"The one I was in was like a fucking mansion. They had so much stuff to break."

"Wow," he says. "Wow. This is…"

"I know, so fucked up."

"Pretty cool," he says at the same time as me.

"What?"

"You're telling me these aliens are going to feed me, clothe me, house me? I never have to work again?"

"Yeah, and they're going to get you all kinds of stupid outfits and little treats and take you for walks, and…"

"Wow," he breathes. "Awesome."

"Dude, what?"

"I was literally about to be homeless," he says. "I lost my job, and my girlfriend kicked me out. I've spent the last two weeks wearing this suit, trying to get a job, watching short videos about living on the street, and now I get a house, free food, and treats?"

Ah hell, I throw the guy a bone. "You might get a new girlfriend here. Some of them like to breed us."

A grin spreads across his face. "Sweet!"

"Not sweet. We're prisoners. We have no choice in our lives…"

I try to warn him that if he gets used as a stud, he's not going to get to have a family. He's not going to get to raise his kids. They're more than likely going to take them away when they're a few years old and sell them while they're cute. We are not people to these creatures.

He listens for half a sentence before he interrupts. "I never had much of a choice in my life anyway. Did you? I got born into a family I didn't choose, got raised in a way I didn't choose, had things happen to me I didn't choose..."

"Okay, Plato," I say, picking a philosopher at random. "Free will might be an illusion, but don't you at least want the illusion?"

"Not really," he says. "Sounds to me like every single problem I ever had just got fixed."

I don't know what else to say, so I don't say anything else. This guy doesn't understand that he's lost everything that really matters. Sure, it might sound good, but it's not. It's just not. He'll realize that sooner or later. He'll see that the only thing that matters is freedom, and everything you trade for it is worthless in comparison. I know.

"Now," Arkan says, coming back. "What to do with you?"

He's looking at me, but it's the guy who replies. I wonder what his name is. I doubt he cares. They'll give him a new one in his new home anyway. They called me Fifi. That was actually closer to Jennifer than I would have imagined. Maybe they caught some psychic vibe of my name.

"Mr Alien, sir? Is that family still out there? Will they take me?"

"Eager to be rehomed? Good. Makes for a nice change. Jennifer here isn't a fan of being a pet."

"I am."

"Of course you are. Because you're a good boy. Who is a good boy? You are! Of course you are!" The alien is praising the guy like there's no other guy in the universe and the dude is absolutely soaking it up. He's just been turned from a free man into a commodity, and he doesn't care. Some people are beyond saving, I guess.

Arkan opens the cage and lifts the man out, carrying the full-grown dude the same way humans carry little dogs, under his arm like he weighs absolutely fucking nothing.

That'll be the last time I see that guy. He's going to a home the size of a small apartment building back on Earth. He'll have a bowl with the name Fifi written on it and a comfortable bed under the stairs. He'll shit in a box, and he'll probably like it.

"The males of your species are often much more sensible than the females," Arkan observes when he returns. "I think he will be a much more suitable pet for that family. You, on the other hand, are going to take a little more training. I think it's time I took you home."

I've never been anywhere other than out the back of his store. I wonder if his home is worse than this. I wonder if anywhere is worse than this. I don't think so.

"I don't want to go to your stinking home. Let me go back to my home."

"Your planet is dying," he reminds me. "Every human I take from your world is another human that doesn't have to suffer. I'm singlehandedly saving your species, potentially, from extinction."

"We didn't ask for you to save us. And we definitely didn't ask you to sell us. Jerk."

Arkan's cool, calm facade is starting to crack. I've cost him money, probably. He wanted to sell two of us and he's only been able to sell one. He'll have to make another run back to Earth to scoop some more of us up, and when he does that, I'll be ready. I have two plans. One of them is to sneak onboard his human thieving ship and hitchhike my way back to Earth. The other option is even better.

"You've got a hell of an attitude for someone who was starving when I found her. You're still underweight."

"Fuck off, I am not."

"You didn't eat what they fed you," he says. "They told me you refused practically everything they gave you. You will eat what I give you."

"Or what?"

He fixes me with a stern alien stare. "Or I will discipline you."

"I'll bite you, and you know my mouth is full of all sorts of nasty human germs. You might get sick. You might have to go to the hospital. I bit one of the aliens and they went to the hospital."

"I know. They told me. And then I covered their bill."

"Wow, that was dumb of you."

He gives me an indulgent but stern look. "You were not ready to be sold. It was an accident. I do not know that you would ever be suitable as a pet. You lack the ability to be comfortable."

"What is that supposed to mean?"

"It means that even provided with the means to be happy, you cannot be happy."

I know he said he was going to punish me, but I never thought he'd hit that deep.

"That's cold."

"It's the truth." He gives me a look that penetrates all the way to the very core of all my fucked up problems and places, the parts of me I've tried to hide. I hate that he's so perceptive. I'd say it's just because he's an alien, but the other aliens had no fucking idea what to do with me. He seems to know exactly what to do with me.

As soon as I have that thought, he proves me correct.

"Before I transport you, you need to have a taste of what's coming when you act out. You are absolutely not going to get away with a single thing you did to that poor family, and I am not going to tolerate your human insolence."

He opens the cage door and I step out. His threats mean very little to me. I know he won't hurt me. Can't break the merchandise, after all. Even the aliens I spent the last week tormenting didn't hurt me. I'm worth too much in this fucked up alien economy to suffer any real consequences.

At least, that's what I thought. When he reaches for me and starts to pull me toward him, I wonder if I've made the wrong assumption. He sits down in the chair he usually sits in when he is going to do his alien paperwork, or conduct what seems to be a longer range conversation in his head. Telepathy is very strange to be around. Seeing aliens fight without saying so much as a word is wild. I know this because the husband and wife aliens who took me home did nothing but fight the entire time I was there. Stony stares and haughty glances interspersed with occasional gasps and yowls of pain when I bit them were the order of the day.

"I've observed methods of discipline among humans. This is old-fashioned, but I believe it could be effective with you, as appeals to reason and sense have had little effect. You are going to get a spanking, pet."

More tart zingers zip across my ego, skimming the surface of what I am. I feel very naked, though I am still clothed in the ridiculous pet outfit my last alien owners provided me. His final threat sends a pulse of heat through me just from the words alone.

A spanking.

I've never gotten one. Never had an authority figure who noticed me long enough to give me one. Growing up at the end of the world is not an easy thing. Never knew my father, and my mom, well, she had bigger things to worry about. This is the first time I have ever been over anybody's knee, and Arkan's alien size makes me feel small enough without the position itself contributing.

Arkan pulls me over his big alien thighs and I know he is going to make good on the promise he just made. Instead of going directly sideways over his lap, I find myself pulled up and over it in a sort of diagonal.

I knew there would be consequences for my alien rampage. I just didn't know that they would be so exciting. My thighs are spread on either side of one of his legs, my pussy grinding against his alien muscle. I feel little pulses of excitement radiating out from that filthy fulcrum he has created.

"Don't do this," I say, though my head is just sort of dangling near the floor, and I have all the authority of a lesser animal. Arkan hasn't listened to a fucking word I said since I met him, why would he start listening now?

"I am going to take you home, and at my home, I expect you to obey me. Every time you act out, rebel against my rules, behave yourself like a bad little pet, I will spank you. Hard. I will make you feel the painful consequences of your actions. I will teach you how to behave, and I will show you how to be happy."

With that damn near sweet sentiment, he starts spanking my ass fast and hard, his big alien palm going from one cheek to the other with swift accuracy. My skin stings and aches and I feel a flush of pure outrage and humiliation. How dare he? How... fuck... how am I going to withstand this? I've never been spanked before. I've been hit before. I've had my ass kicked before, but this feels different. I don't get a chance to fight this. And he's not doing it out of anger, or hatred, or anything like that. He's doing it because he wants me to be better. To behave better. He wants me to obey him, and that's why my ass is now blazing hot.

I hate every second of it, but I cannot escape. This alien, unlike the others, knows how to hold and restrain human without hurting them. That means I am pinned in place over his big alien lap, and every single one of the many dozens of perfectly calibrated slaps designed to sting and humiliate me lands precisely where he intends them to.

My wails are ones of outrage more than pain, though there's plenty of sensation to complain about. It feels as though my entire rear has been turned into a hot plate radiating fiery intensity through the entirety of my body. As much as I want to continue to growl and snarl, there are whimpers there as well, escaping my lips and making their way to his ears.

He slows a little, then stops, laying his hand across both of my cheeks. His touch is almost comforting, but it comes far too late to truly soothe me.

"I know this hurts," he says. "And I know it makes you furious to be punished, but this is what you need. Pleasure and pain. Consequence and reward. This is how you will become happy and settled, knowing that your world makes sense, is predictable and safe."

I don't want to hear it. I want him to let me fucking go. I want to be off his knee, and away from his punishing palm. So I do what any trapped animal would do with only limited ways to escape.

I bite him. One of his hands is on my ass, but the other one has brushed past my face, moving my hair away from my gaze. I latch onto his middle and pointer finger, biting down as hard as I can in the effort to make him release me.

There's a loud curse and a jerk as he registers his own dose of punishing pain. I buck hard in the attempt to escape, planning to dash out the back of the store, through the main body of the shop, and out into the street. His grip does loosen for a moment, but not enough for my squirming to make a difference.

I wait for him to say something, but he doesn't make so much as a sound. Instead, his palm explodes against my ass, a flurry of harsh slaps beating across my ass in a thunderous tattoo.

"You do NOT bite," he growls at me, suddenly very stern. "You will never do that again. I know you've done that to the family, but after today, I promise that will not be something you consider."

No more Mr Nice Alien, I guess.

There's the sound of a couple snaps unsnapping, and then I feel a sudden cool breeze on my ass. He's pulled the seat of my bodysuit open and now has unfettered access to my bare rear. The realization makes me tense up all the more, which is about the worst thing I could do right before a thin wood or maybe plastic implement whips across my ass. The feeling is akin to being snapped with a line of pure fire. It doesn't have the weight and heft of his palm, but it stings like crazy, and Arkan wastes no time in whipping it against my ass dozens of times in a row, giving me no quarter whatsoever.

He's so fucking mean. He's completely ruthless. And he's absolutely intent on making sure I know I cannot cross him.

I might be starting to get the idea.

. . .

Arkan

This wayward brat of a human is finally learning a long-overdue lesson. Her cheeks are nicely marked, but not so much that she cannot take more. I will return to punishing them again, but first I want to address the use of her teeth more directly. She has no shame or reluctance whatsoever when it comes to biting, and that is going to stop today.

I grasp my writhing little ballerina and pull her up to her feet. She might think this means her punishment is over. She would be wrong. She's far from the first human to bite me, and I have developed ways and means of dealing with that tendency. The most effective is to introduce an unpleasant object to her mouth while her bottom is still hot and stinging.

I keep a small supply of bite inhibitors on the shelves next to my desk. It is not difficult to take one of them and bring it to her nose.

"This is a bar of saponified fats," I tell her, keeping a firm grip on the back of her neck. My scaled hand nearly completely encircles her throat. When this is done, she will wear my collar and she will experience a level of obedience and submission that she cannot begin to imagine right now. For the moment, she squirms and wriggles in my grasp, not so much trying to escape as merely reacting to the sensations flooding her punished flesh.

"Looks like soap..."

With those fateful words, she opens her mouth wide enough for me to slip the bar inside.

Her reaction is one of immediate disgust and of course to attempt to escape the unpleasant but harmless taste. As much as she wriggles, I keep the pressure on, ensuring that the foaming soap covers her tongue and fills her mouth with a taste that will not soon be forgotten.

When it comes to biting, the habit must be stopped abruptly and immediately the moment it happens. There can be no mercy, no quiet talks, and no gentle handling.

I hold the soap in her mouth, and I lecture her sternly. "You do not bite. Not anybody. Not ever. Not me. Not anyone else. Do you understand?"

There are bubbles emerging from her mouth as she swiftly nods, giving up all pretense of fight as she chooses obedience over soap. It is good to know that she is capable of giving to pressure. I was starting to think she might be one of the rare breeds of human with no capacity for regard for consequences. Some people can be punished past the point of all sense and still have absolutely no tendency to change their behavior.

This is not my pet's problem. She is simply stubborn and spoiled and has never met a consequence until this moment.

The expression in her big brown eyes is exquisite. Truly beautiful. Tears are gathering in a misty haze, making her eyes bright. She is holding back those tears, but only just. I can see other emotions too, confusion, and perhaps even gratitude. There must be some small part of her that is relieved to have finally met someone who will not allow her to act as she pleases all the time.

Finally, I pull the soap from her mouth and point to a corner of my office where the desk meets the bare wall before guiding her to the spot where I want her to be. She takes the few steps I want and then stands quite still. The seat of her bodysuit is still lowered, revealing her bright red cheeks. I take a moment to place her hands on her head, palms down, one over the other.

"Stand there and stay," I order.

To her credit, or perhaps to the credit of shock and awe, she does stay there for a good minute or two, completely still, her shoulders shaking just a little with the sobs she refuses to let out.

I sit back on my chair and watch her, this brief moment of almost serene obedience. I know what she is like. I know she is chaotic and rebellious, and I know that this punishment will wear off and she will return to that state. But something will have been learned in between. The next time her jaws begin to part with the intention of biting, she will still them for at least a moment. Hesitation will become part of her experience of disobedience rather than unconsidered impulsive action.

After a short time, she begins to squirm. It is inevitable. She is uncomfortable and emotional. Her body is awash with chemical impulses and old thought patterns vying for control in this new situation. I hear slight vocalizations emerging from her. She wants to speak disrespectfully. She wants to yell and curse and throw her relatively diminutive weight around.

She does none of it, and once another few short seconds pass, I retrieve her from the corner. I do not want to push her past the point of her limited capacity for obedience. I want to keep her right there and give her relief at the moment she was most submissive.

"You are going to wash that soap out of your mouth now," I tell her. "And you are going to keep your teeth for eating and nothing else. Understand?"

I get a brief, evasive nod. She does not want to look at me. She is ashamed, not of her bad behavior, but of her submission. It is a humiliation to a creature like this to bend her will in any way to that of another. I will have to ensure there are abundant awards for obedience if I am to truly make her mine.

There is a water supply in all the human cages. I let her go and make use of the one she was just in, trying not to appear too amused as she splashes and splutters in the effort to remove all traces of soap from the inside of her mouth. It is an effort doomed to fail. She will be tasting that punishment for quite some time.

When she has as much of the soap out of her mouth as possible, she looks at me with an ever-so-slightly chastened expression.

"Are we done?"

"Far from it, little one. Come here."

Her face falls, and I see temptation to disobedience written clearly on her features. She wants to defy me, but even as her eyes dart about the room she can see that there is no escape. She can obey me, or she can disobey me, and either way she will suffer the consequences.

Her feet take slow steps as she delivers herself to me. The outfit her erstwhile owners chose for her does not suit her, but in this particular moment it does lend a certain vulnerability.

She's very cute. But she's much naughtier than she is cute.

I take her by the hand once she is in range and draw her back over my lap. She lets me take her over my thighs with a soft sob and lies almost like a tamed pet in place. I spread my palm over her cheeks, feel the deserved heat, and swat her lightly.

Jen

My mouth tastes like soap, my ass feels like it's made of lava, and I don't know what's happened to me. I am lying over Arkan's thighs, letting him spank my already whipped ass and not even trying to destroy him.

He's done something to me that I didn't think was possible. He's made me compliant. I don't even feel like biting him, or scratching him, or calling him the worst thing I can possibly concoct in my mind. It's such a strange feeling, I'd almost wonder if I'd been drugged if I hadn't experienced every painful stroke and foam of his punishment firsthand.

At least he is being more gentle now. The slaps are not as punitive, and his tone when he speaks is softer.

"I think you're already starting to feel what is on the other side of obedience, pet," he purrs gently, stroking and rubbing my very sore rear with careful motions. "This doesn't have to hurt. None of it does. If you can behave, you will be happy. I promise you that."

My eyelids are heavy. Maybe this is okay. Maybe…

The memory of a world far from this one returns to my mind. Harsh words, rough actions, a life of struggle and toil. He wants to take that all away from me. He wants to make my life easy. All I have to do is submit to him and whoever he sells me to, and...

Fuck. That.

It is a real effort to rouse myself from the comfortable state of dreamy submission he has put me into. I am fighting my body and many parts of my mind. But fight I must.

"Settle down," he says soothingly.

"Let me fucking go," I growl.

There's a brief pause and maybe something like a sigh. "Back to your feisty self are you, pet?" His tone is not overly concerned, or surprised.

"I'm my own person. I'm not your pet. Now let me up and let me go, or I will..." I search my mind for threats. "I will ruin this world."

"The world?" He chuckles. "You're going to ruin the entire world, are you, pet?"

He doesn't take me seriously. He should.

Arkan ignores my post-punishment cursing and growling as he puts me back inside my travel crate with my ass burning and my pride bruised. These aliens have a way of making a person truly feel like a pet, and I know that appeals to some, like the guy he just resold after having captured him five minutes ago. But it doesn't appeal to me. I burn with a desire to manifest my own goddamn destiny. There is a part of me that is forever animal, properly wild and free in spite of shackles, cages, and spankings.

Looking out through bars offends that part of me deeply. I was not born to live in a cage. I was not made to be a pet. I am a wild fucking animal, and I intend to keep acting like it no matter what Arkan and his crew of advanced alien customers do.

Maybe if I act badly enough, I'll get humans banned, the way certain dog breeds used to be banned back on Earth before everybody had bigger things to worry about. Anything to make a difference in the lives of others. I'll be as terrible as I can be in service of humanity.

Arkan picks me up, cage and all, and hefts me into the back of his transport vehicle. There aren't many wheeled vehicles on this world, but his is an exception. I guess it's like a pickup truck with a big back deck. My crate is put on that deck, and then fastened with straps.

"Be good," Arkan says, tapping the crate. He then walks away, gets in the truck, and sets off for wherever home is.

This world is rich. The city I'm in spans mile upon mile over what seems to be largely flat terrain. They like to build up in big spiral-type buildings, large at the base and tapering up as they get taller. Almost all of them have exterior walkways around the outside of them, and a lot of those walkways link up with other buildings, creating a massive city-wide network of paths suspended hundreds of feet in the air.

Arkan's little human pet shop is located in an older area of the city, in what humans would call the outskirts if this was a human city. There are cobble-style streets and little houses and shops. It's adorable and quaint and the vibe is somewhere between ye olde cottage and 1950's wholesome. I needed to get myself returned here, not because of this location, but because of what this location is somewhat adjacent to: the wilderness.

I noticed when I was first brought here that out beyond the sprawl of older housing and shops is a verdant, thick forest. These aliens have created a very dense city that fits many millions of them inside it, but they've also apparently left large swathes of their home world untouched.

This is where my second plan comes in. I've always dreamed of living out in nature, away from other people, and especially away from other aliens. I'm drawn by the prospect of solitude and freedom, away from obligation to anybody. Arkan thinks he's offering me a perfect life because I'd be taken care of, and on one level, sure. Not having to provide for myself inside a capitalist structure of commerce and trade is attractive on some level. The idea of just being an animal living wild, not beholden to a system that takes what we're all entitled to forage for ourselves, and turns it into commodities we must grind our very lives to the literal bone for.

My plan was to leave the city and go into the wilds back on Earth, but it was hard. Most of the wilderness was toxic, and what wasn't was covered in tiny houses in various states of disarray. Vicious van lifers roamed the forests, beaches, highways, byways, and anything remotely drivable in small packs, stopping only to dance to viral beats from time to time. They had started out as peaceful people, escaping society, but over time they naturally evolved into small tribes raiding other tribes for spare tires, cute storage options, and life-hacks.

Point is, when an entire world is broken, there's nowhere to run. But this alien world is not broken, and here I have some chance of a true escape, home-free.

Arkan

That was quite a punishment. It was also quite a recovery from a punishment. I cannot imagine how hard she had to fight herself to reclaim her defiance so quickly. Most pets, once punished, like to be caressed and comforted for quite some time afterward, reassured that they are still good.

But nothing is easy with this one. It is entirely possible that it never will be easy with her. I've caught hundreds of humans over the years, and though some have to be rehomed after their first sale in order to find an owner who truly suits them, I've never had an outright return for bad behavior. Most humans quickly realize that they have fallen on their feet in our world once they have a comfortable bed and as much food as they care to eat. Our species treats humans with a certain reverence and compassion, acknowledging their place in the chain of evolution. They may be simple beasts who cannot speak mind to mind, but they are part of a cosmic heritage, a lineage from which we all descend in one way or another.

Jennifer is an exquisite specimen, as beautiful as she is temperamentally strange. I find the way her eyes flash pure fire at me, and the sheer loathing she seems to be holding onto quite uncommon. Most humans come pre-tamed, broken by their own systems. They are usually grateful for food, shelter, protection, for never having to make another decision in their lives.

She's trouble, but she's also very pretty. We do not mate outside our species, but there are rumors that some human females, and indeed males, have made intimate companions for our kind. I, of course, have never mated the merchandise, and I do not encourage it. But suddenly, I understand it.

I wish she was not back in the deck in her cage. I'd like to have her ride in the front seat beside me. I'd like to talk to her about her life before this moment and explain what awaits her on this world. I'd like to see her purr instead of hiss and growl. But for now, I know she'd probably leap from the moving vehicle the very first chance she got.

I want to tame her.

There's a challenge to this human I haven't encountered before. I know it won't be easy. I don't want to break her spirit. I just want to break through this untrusting exterior and see her soft. I want her to feel safe with me. I want everything every pet owner wants, for his pet to be happy.

I do know this: there's no chance of selling her again. Not now she's gone and bitten someone. If the authorities discover that, they'll impound and destroy her. She's a liability. A danger. And she's mine.

I should have known it when I captured her...

A *few Earth days ago...*

Hidden from the view of the people scurrying below me, I sit in my cloaked shuttle and watch the city humans, looking for one or perhaps two who might make suitable pets.

I am looking for a very specific sort of human. One who is not connected strongly to a familial group. Humans become very distressed if you accidentally take a mother or a father. Their young suffer terribly, so I never take any human who has previously bred. This is obvious in the pheromone readings. I have my drone probes flitting through the streets, taking samples from those who pass by, alerting me to any potentials. This gives me time to cast my gaze over this section of the ruined city.

Once upon a time, this was a proud city. Now it is a haven of decay and depravity. Law, such as it is, is enforced sporadically and with great violence. Crime is ubiquitous.

And yet, life finds a way to limp on. In the burned-out shells of what used to be mass retail outlets, peddlers and scavengers sell their wares. They attempt to emulate old styles of commerce with handmade banners and sales pitches. Almost all of them are armed to the teeth with improvised weapons. Seen in a certain distant and rose-colored light, there is a certain cheerfulness to the entire proceedings.

But the people are not well. They are suffering and they are in danger. For every successful trade, there is a raid from a thief and perhaps a small band thereof.

Young males roam the bullet pock-marked streets in large groups. These groups harass others, and when they encounter other groups, large fights break out that leave some dead, many maimed, and all traumatized.

A law enforcement cruiser slides silently and unseeingly past a man who is on the ground being kicked by three youths who asked him if he had a cigarette, then proceeded to beat him when he said he did not.

The man on the ground survives only because he has secreted a handheld incendiary device in his pocket. I watch, fascinated, as he deploys it in a thin stream of what looks to be very unpleasantly hot fire. Their screams make the microphones on my drone probes rattle unpleasantly.

Once upon a time I used to try to intervene in these scuffles, but I quickly discovered the law of unintended consequences, not to mention it becoming absolutely impossible to police. I have a permit to capture humans in the wild, but I am not permitted to intervene in the progress of their civilization in general.

I refocus my probes. At the moment there is great demand for young adult females. One such human is owned by one of the most influential families on Euphoria, and as such, the type has become most sought after.

The problem with finding humans of this type is that young adult females very rarely venture out into the streets of this or any other city. They are kept indoors for their own safety, for all social conventions have eroded over time. The same bands of youths who set upon men will snatch women if given the chance.

I have to hope to catch a female when she leaves the safety of cover to scuttle for fresh cover.

Appearing almost as if on cue, my probes detect a female. Most of them move swiftly, with their heads down and their hair and faces covered in the futile attempt to avoid the ravaging male gaze. She does not bother. She strides out into the street with purpose and a hint of aggression.

My probes sweep toward her and begin relaying biodata. First of all, I note that she has not bred. That is an excellent start. Her hair has been colored a bright reddish pink not found in nature. In many Earth animals, bright colors announce danger to others. I can only imagine that this serves the same purpose. Her rather sweet face is set in a determined scowl. Probe data reveals she appears to be in her mid-twenties, and not currently in her breeding window.

Men look at her with interest as she strides past, but they do not approach, sensing the hostility she emanates. It is a pity, but I know she is not a good candidate for captivity. Something about her is wild through and through. As much as I might personally be intrigued, my brothers and I long ago agreed that we would not take any humans we could not sell. The Pet Shop is a business, and we must run it like one. The temptation to have our own pets must be resisted.

A good pet is someone with a softer temperament, someone who will take well to being looked after. I usually select from the lower ranked humans I encounter. They are usually not much to look at when they are first captured. I take them filthy, sick, and broken, and I rehabilitate them until they are gleaming with health and happiness.

Regretfully letting that target go, I refocus my attention to humans elsewhere in the target area. There are quite a number of them. There's a promising looking male, strongly built with red hair. Natural red hair has become quite popular back on Euphoria. He does not have any of the obvious markers of having fathered offspring, though it is harder to tell with the males. Their overall contribution to the species is biologically limited to the act of orgasm.

I am supposed to be looking for a female, but there's no reason I can't take a good specimen like him too. There are several berths in my ship, and I'd like to fill them all before I leave. I have a waiting list of homes for anything I catch. Trade is good. Life is good.

I prepare the capture sequence, which involves releasing a cloud of psychogenic dust throughout the area, effectively erasing the senses of those close enough to see what happens. The second stage of capture happens when I deploy a tractor beam, effectively plucking the human from the surface of the planet and sucking them into my shuttle. Once I have a freshly caught human on board my shuttle, the psychogenic dust keeps them quiet long enough to get them back to the ship.

"Get your fucking hands off me!"

I hear female distress, and when I refocus my attention, I find that it is the woman who first caught my eye. She has gained the attention of three males, all of whom are emitting threatening mating pheromones.

They have cornered her in an alley, each and every one of them twice her size. They are grabbing at her, initiating coarse sexual contact without her interest or consent.

She jabs at one with her knee, making contact with the part of his anatomy he would like to bury inside her. It is a very effective strike.

He groans and collapses.

One of his friends attempts to help him. The other strikes the female across her face with an open hand and grabs her by the throat with his other. He threatens to kill her.

I am too far away to physically intervene, and I have never set foot on the planet before. But I can help, even though I shouldn't. A thousand travesties and cruelties take place every second in this city. But my fingers are already at work.

ZIP!

I activate the transport beam, and the human is removed from the situation, beamed from that filthy alley all the way to my shuttle.

"GET YOUR FUCKING HANDS OFF ME, YOU FUCK..."

I turn around to find the human in the small confines on the shuttle, safe and sound, but gasping for air, a red ring of human hand around her throat. Because there was no time to release the dust, she is not sedated. She is aware of absolutely everything that just happened to her, and she is not happy about any of it. Far from being relieved to find herself rescued, she is clearly still flooded with adrenaline and ready to fight.

She turns around, looks at me, and I brace myself for what feels like the inevitable scream. Humans almost always shriek when they see me for the first time. I am an intimidating creature, much larger than they are, and impossibly strange. My lower tusks cause significant consternation in most cases.

The human stares at me, her eyes sweeping down my body and then back up to my eyes.

"The fuck are you?"

The question is succinct and sounds faintly offended. I detect no discernible fear at all. I suppose I am not accosting her, so compared to her immediately previous circumstances she is much safer.

"My name is Arkan," I explain. "I am a merchant and human trainer. I am not intending to hurt you."

"Human trainer? What the fuck is happening?"

She is still charged with adrenaline, terrified, agitated, and ready to fight. I wonder if I should provide a little in the way of sedation, but I want to inspect her and make sure that she was not harmed by the brutes who attacked her, and I want to talk to her.

I set the controls of the shuttle to send it skimming back to the main ship. I need to get her safely contained before she becomes unruly. This human has unruly all over her. She needs a bath too. Not because she is particularly personally dirty, but because the stench of the human city clings to her. It smells like smoke and toxic waste mixed with plastic micro-particles and petrochemicals. They do love to burn things down there. If something can be set on fire, a human will set fire to it.

Her clothing has seen better days. The leggings are ripped and torn horizontally across her thighs and knees. She's wearing a light piece of fabric that does little to cover much of her upper body, and a great deal of strapping that is studded and clearly designed to mimic the spiky plumage of certain animals on their planet. She is a study in attraction and repulsion.

I have the urge to bathe her and replace these sweaty, dirty scraps with a nice, cozy onesie suit that will cover her more modestly, and much more comfortably for that matter. I have had these suits designed from an absorbent and soft material that humans seem to find very comforting to be encased in.

"I noticed that you were in distress," I tell her. "What is your name?"

"Jennifer," she says, spitting the word as if it is an insult to me somehow. To say she is combative is an understatement, but she is still recovering from combat, so that makes sense.

"Would you like something to eat, Jennifer?"

I never go near a human without a bar of chocolate. Having harvested cacao seeds from the planet, I've made a point of having a small plantation back home in order to be able to manufacture organic chocolate treats for humans. It is the one substance that almost all of them will obey for and makes the training process much more smooth.

She perks up at the offer.

"Is that chocolate?"

"Yes."

She lunges for the bar, clearly intending on consuming the entire thing at once. I have no intention of allowing that, so I pull it away before she has a chance of snatching it away.

"You may have a piece," I tell her as she comes to an abrupt and offended halt before me. "But I need you to sit down first, please."

She takes a seat in my chair, throwing her leg over one of the arms, looking immediately and completely at home.

"Not there," I smile. "On the floor."

"On the... why?" She challenges me immediately.

"I need my chair in order to continue to pilot the shuttle, and there is not a second chair, so in terms of securing you as best as possible, the floor is it. Unless, of course, you'd like to sit in my lap."

I watch a hot flush of red rise up through her skin. I like that. She is responding to me on a basic chemical level, which means she is open to me.

She doesn't say a word, just gets up and stands at her rather limited full height, arms folded over her chest in what I recognize as a self-protective gesture.

"I would like you to sit down," I say.

"I'm not sitting on the fucking floor."

"Then I can't give you the chocolate, I'm afraid."

This is about more than a sweet treat. This is about starting her training while she is hungry. It is not easy to survive in the human world, and it is even harder to obtain treats. The chocolate I have to offer her represents a very high value reward.

I am pleased to see her cross her legs at the ankles and sink toward the floor, sitting in a cross-legged position with her arm and hand stuck out toward me.

"Give," she says.

I give her three pieces, which is a generous allotment. I want her to know that I am where food and comfort comes from. Once she begins to look to my kind, any of the Euphorians, for sustenance and affection, she will be mostly tamed.

Jennifer puts the entire chunk into her mouth, chews and swallows within a few seconds. She then proceeds to stand up again, resetting the behavior in the transparent attempt to gain more chocolate.

"Sit," I repeat.

She does as she's told with a smirk on her face. I give her another three pieces of chocolate. She thinks she is getting away with something, but in truth she is already becoming trained.

I may have been mistaken. She may turn out to be a fine pet after all. Her attitude will soften, and perhaps over time she will become quite content.

She gets up again, then sits again before I ask her to sit. Another three pieces of chocolate, another smirk from her.

It is safe to say that she is not harmed from her altercation on Earth. The mark around her neck will remain for some time and probably bruise. The males were rough with her. I shudder to think what fate might have befallen her if she had been left to their merciless perversions. Humans were once regarded as semi-civilized, but that is no longer the case. Many of them now give into the most primitive, animal instincts, caring nothing for the law or for anyone else.

I work with Jen, performing initial training all the way back to the ship, letting her take the majority of the bar of chocolate off me in a series of small obediences.

There's a slight *clunk* when we dock, and that means it is time to put her into storage for the duration of the journey.

"Alright," she says, seeming to sense the transition. "When do I get to go home?"

"I'm afraid you do not. I intend to take you to my home world, Euphoria, where you will be taken care of from this day until your very last."

"The hell I am. I need to get back home. Thanks for the chocolate, but I have things to do. I was in the middle of a jigsaw puzzle."

I happen to know what a jigsaw puzzle is, and I do not believe for a second that it is such a pastime that draws her back to the planet. Humans are often convinced that they have important matters to attend to in their lives, but absent dependent infants, I do not acknowledge them. Anything she might have happening in the life that made her so filthy and put her at such risk is unimportant compared to the life that awaits her.

"I am sorry," I say. "But what lies ahead of you is a life of comfort..."

I do not get a chance to finish my sentence, because the docking process has opened the lock between the shuttle and the ship, and her presence close to the door has caused the sensor to register as someone it should open for.

She takes off running into my ship. I give chase. There are plenty of things inside the vessel that are not safe for a loose human to encounter. She's faster than I expect her to be and agile around corners.

She manages to get all the way to the bridge before I grab her. On the way, I picked a small dose of sedative from my pocket. I know better than to allow loose humans on a shuttle or ship. The fact that she's now wailing and shrieking and kicking dangerously close to the control console is my fault.

"Let me go! Take me back home!" She looks at me with wild, panicked eyes. She is afraid merely to be afraid. If she stopped and thought about it, she would realize she is now far safer than she has ever been. She is not capable of thinking, however. Her brain is in a state designed only for survival and escape. This is why I need the sedative. No logic or kindness will overcome this panic. She needs time, space, and the opportunity to process her new life.

"I am going to take you home," I tell her. "It will be a new home, but you'll love it just as much as this one, and probably a good deal more."

With that, I pump a few sprites of human pheromones and a good dose of sedative into her face. The deep and panicked breaths she's taking draw it all into her system and she goes immediately completely floppy.

I carry her to my human cargo hold. When I return from these trips, it is full of prime human stock. There is one bay left for this pretty young human. Most of the other bays are occupied by sedated, slumbering pets sleeping peacefully in cozy beds. Everybody will be comfortable and happy all the way to Euphoria. I settle my newest little captive into her bay, a small area with a bed and enough area to stand up, turn around, and lie down in. If my sedation protocol is effective, she will stay asleep until...

No sooner have I shut the door than her eyes flick open. I am shocked for a second. I've never seen a human wake up, certainly not that quickly.

"You think you can drug me down? You think you can put me out with a spray?" She pops up out of the bed, hands on hips, and glares at me with those furious dark eyes. "You better open this cage and let me go home, alien, or you are going to regret it."

"I can't open it. It's not safe for you. I can give you another dose of sedative, or you can take a nap of your own accord. But you are not coming out of there until we are back on Euphoria."

She draws her foot back and kicks the door hard enough to make the entire pod shudder. Fortunately, the other inhabitants are deep in slumber and do not stir. She can throw all the tantrums she likes in there.

My newest human acquisition is absolutely beside herself with rage. She begins to threaten me at the top of her lungs, her shouts muted by the thick walls of her translucent prison.

"I'm going to fuck your shit up, alien. I'm going to burn your world to the fucking ground if you take me there."

I can understand her anger, though I would have thought she'd manage a little more in the way of gratitude. If I had not swept her up when I did, she would have been seriously hurt. I know that one gallant action does not make me any less of a predator stalking their failing world, but I hope to become a rescuer to those I do save.

"It's okay," I tell her. "You are safe."

"Fuck you."

I draw a phrase from the depths of human history, the only possible response in this situation. She deserves discipline, and she will get it, but for now, while she is in transit, she can stay in her pod.

"Alrighty then."

3

Jen

Wind blows past me and my ridiculous fucking tutu as I huddle in the back of the crate to stay out of the elements as much as is possible, cursing Arkan and his interference in my life. Thanks to his punishment, sitting down is almost impossible, so I find myself crouched and braced in a very undignified position as we wind our way through the idyllic old city, and to my very great excitement, into the countryside.

I smell wild air, scented with unfamiliar flowers. I see trees and fields passing on either side of a very bumpy and poorly maintained dirt road. I have to brace myself over a divot or two in particular, before he slows down, realizing that his precious cargo is being rattled about in the back like a rock in a tin can.

He'll regret this. He'll regret everything.

He turns off what barely passes for a road, down a long and winding driveway. It is bordered by verdant trees and rutted with the passage of many vehicles. The world smells different here. There is earth, dirt, plant detritus, animal things. It is an alien smell, but it is also one that hits somewhere deep in my core because this is the smell from which we all came. I was born in the city. I've never touched grass before, but seeing the bright bloom of it fills me with hope of a kind that feels alien to me.

I should be mad as hell. I *am* mad as hell. But I'm something else too, now. I'm curious, and my lungs are full of the kind of air that plants just got done excreting and it feels like there's this buzzing, blooming existence happening all around me and in me, and maybe I'm a part of it.

Never thought I'd feel at home on an alien world, not even a little bit. The truck jolts again and I just narrowly stop my head from hitting the top of the crate as we come to a halt at what has to be Arkan's house. The vehicle is parked away from the house, so my view is mostly of the path along which we just came.

Arkan gets out and walks around to the crate to check on me.

"Fuck off," I say, assuring him that all is well with me.

He exhales slightly impatiently and walks over to the gate we just came through, shutting it firmly. From what I can see, there is quite a tall fence around the entirety of the property made of a rock and cement situation. Almost looks like some of the old Earth buildings. Kind of charming. Am I starting to not hate every second of this experience? I hope not. I don't want to become tame. I've seen too many tame humans, and they make me sick with the way they follow their owners around.

I remember the first time I met another owned human. It was two days ago. My owner wanted to show off his new purchase at a fancy alien gathering of some kind. A birthday party, maybe. I don't know exactly because nobody told me.

All of a sudden I was in a big room with more aliens than I'd ever imagined. My new owner didn't have a leash or a collar on me. He seemed to think I'd just stay with him, like some kind of sentient Roomba.

T*wo days ago....*

I wander away from my alien owner, looking for a way out of this party and off this planet. My plan has not changed since I was captured. I intend to get back home. I'm not a fucking commodity. I'm a person, and I own myself.

The crowd of formally dressed aliens parts for a brief moment, and my heart skips a beat when I see another human. There is a young woman around my age with flowing blonde hair that looks like it has been brushed a thousand times, slightly wispy around her head and shoulders. She is wearing a golden gown, a smaller version of the one her alien mistress is wearing. A collar encircles her throat, and a light golden leash connects her to the wrist of her alien owner.

She looks up at her owner as I approach, and the alien woman unclips her leash. There does not seem to be any animosity between them. I have to assume the other human is playing for time, pretending to play along with the alien agenda before making good her escape.

"Hello," she says in a soft whisper voice that is barely audible. "My name is Melinda. What's yours?"

She extends her hand to me, almost as if to go for a handshake, but flopping her wrist more like I'm supposed to kiss her freakin' hand. I ignore the motion and step closer to her.

"How the fuck do we get out of here, Melinda?"

She gives me a strange look, as if my question is uncouth and very strange. She takes a step back, putting distance between us, and glancing back at her alien mistress as if for comfort.

"I'm sure I don't know what you mean."

Her accent makes me think she's from the other side of the Atlantic, but that's no excuse to be unaware of the horrors being visited upon us as a whole. We're captives, people being traded for the entertainment of aliens.

"I mean, how do we get out of here?"

She gives a little shrug, as if the matter holds no interest to her.

I watch, stunned, as the female alien walks by, pets Melinda on the head, and drops a treat from between pale, scaled fingers. Melinda catches what looks like a boiled sweet and performs an actual fucking curtsey.

Melinda now speaks to me softly around her little sweet treat, changing the subject to one she is capable of engaging with.

"My owners are very high up in the government," she says, smirking at me as if their achievement is hers.

"Okay," I say blankly.

"What does your owner do?"

I knew that question was coming somehow.

"I have no fucking idea. And I couldn't begin to care."

She looks me up and down, judging my attire, which is outlandish and ridiculous, but not as fancy as hers.

"By the looks of it, probably a simple merchant. His wife probably works. And I imagine their children go to a common school."

I have no idea what she is talking about, and I have even less interest in finding out.

"Did Kahn sell you?"

She asks another question in that same smug tone that implies she is better than I am. Any hope of getting any useful information out of her is starting to dwindle, but I have to assume she'll eventually accidentally tell me something I can leverage.

"I don't know who Kahn is."

"Kahn sold me. He's one of the brothers who owns the Human Pet Store. The Voros family. They're very influential and incredibly powerful." She speaks the words of that human trading hub with a certain emphasis that implies capital letters and a simpering excitement. "They keep that little shop for appearances, but their family owns half the city, you know. The Wrathelders own the other half. My mistress is a Wrathelder. Jessamine Wrathelder, she's cousin to Phenix, who..."

I cut her off as she embarks on a long tirade of names I neither recognize nor care about. "I was sold by some asshole."

She makes an expression that strongly indicates she does not like my disrespectful tone. Then she keeps talking about the thing she intended on talking about in the first place. "That might have been Arkan. He's good too, but I think Kahn is the best trainer. He's just so elegant. Never rough. Arkan always struck me as far too aggressive."

Of course she thinks her human slave trader is better than the other human slave trader. This woman is under the illusion that she is better than any other human on this, or any other planet. She has fully identified with the role of pet and seems very happy in it.

Gross.

She falls silent once more as the alien woman passes by.

"Are you afraid to speak?"

She shakes her golden head swiftly.

"The aliens don't like it when you speak out loud. It's best to stay silent when you can. They prefer eye contact and signing. Words are very primitive to them. Our speech is like a dog barking. You should learn to lower your voice and speak only when you absolutely have to. It will make your life much easier."

I am deprived of any further pearls of wisdom from Melinda, for her owner returns, clips the leash onto her collar without so much as a word of warning, and proceeds to walk away, leaving Melinda apparently happily trotting in her wake. I am shocked and dismayed.

I am also keen to escape this gathering. It's fortunate that the aliens like an ornate style of dress, especially the women who favor full skirts. It means that if I stoop just a little I am quite quickly hidden in a sea of fabric.

All the heads of the aliens turn in one direction at once as an unspoken word gets their collective attention.

My owner has worked out that he has lost me, and appears to be silently, but rather frantically, asking for help in retrieving me. I'm sure it's not because he cares about me, but because he just spent what seems to be a lot of money on me.

The aliens start to look for me en masse, and I realize there's about ten seconds before one of them grabs me. I do not want to be caught. The nearest door is on the other side of the hall. I think I can make it. There's just one obstacle in the way, a great big long obstacle in the form of the table that holds all the food everybody is shoveling into their mouths.

They spot me.

If this was a group of humans, someone would shout THERE SHE IS! Or GET HER!

But in this group of largely silent aliens, all that happens is several dozen heads swivel toward me at the same time, and a series of eyes lock on me all at once. It is like being spotted by a horde of silent, statuesque, superhuman predators.

Adrenaline spikes, and I decide there's nothing for it. I run and I jump, intending to vault the table and dash down the other side of the room. But the table is taller than I expect it to be. It's made to their scale, not mine. So instead of jumping over it, I sort of fly into it and slide, belly down, through a banquet-length table of delicacies. As I crash through the plates and treats, accumulating a great deal of food on my person, I see a look of pure horror on Melinda's face.

Somewhere in the room, someone makes a faint utterance of surprise. This is now a complete debacle.

If this were a movie, I'd slide down the table, out the doors and forward somersault to freedom. But this is real, and friction means I slide about five feet before coming to a halt more or less inside what used to be a cream cake.

There's silence when I stop, a complete and utter absence of sound broken only by the muffled gasps of Melinda who is trying her very best not to laugh out loud at my misfortune.

The alien who had the misfortune to buy me picks me up off the table, two hands gripping the back of my garment. He is harried and embarrassed. I'm fortunate these aliens aren't given to violence very often. If they were, I know he'd be beating my ass. Instead, he's far too worried about himself. I am carried out of the gathering in the custody of the alien who has purchased my very life, no closer to freedom than I was when I began.

Back at Arkan's house...

I'm starting to think that Arkan and his family are what we used to called old money, back on Earth. Before the rebellion of 202-whatever, when all the billionaires were summarily, let's just say, eaten. Some of what happened to them was better. A lot of it was worse.

"I'm going to open the cage," he says, his eyes flashing with alien warning. "When I do, I'm going to put a leash on you. If you make this hard for me, I will punish you again, and I can promise you it will not feel any better the second time around."

I resolve then and there to bite his hand the second he puts it into my cage. I intend to make this more than hard for him. I am going to make this absolutely impossible for him.

Sure enough, the door of the crate opens, just a crack, enough for him to reach for me. Without hesitation, I latch onto his hand and I bite down hard.

I hear him grunt in pain.

He scruffs me by the back of the neck and hauls me out. I curse him with every foul word I have and some that aren't even coherent sounds.

"You have to make everything difficult, don't you," he rumbles, holding onto me with one hand, and shaking the one I bit. I don't think I broke the scales, but I definitely left a mark of some kind. I feel quite proud of myself for having made an impact on this powerful, fanged creature who has made me a commodity.

He really thought he'd broken me of my bite with the punishment in the pet store. I can see the surprise in his face. He's shocked that his little spanking and his soap treatment didn't make a lasting difference. This guy has dealt with people who break easy. I don't.

Crouched on the deck of the back of his transport, I struggle against his grip. It might not free me, but it is symbolic. I will not give in. Not as long as I have strength in me to fight.

Something catches my eye in my peripheral vision. It is the flash of water from a fountain of the kind that spurts water everywhere. I look around, and the surprise of the entirety of our location stops my struggles as I give into surprise. We are out the front of a huge, classically-designed alien mansion. It is built from big rocks cut square and stacked.... I'm not an architect. It's a fucking mansion, what do you want?

"So this is what you get for selling people, huh? Doing really well for yourself, I see."

"This has been in my family for a thousand years. It is our ancestral home."

"Sure. Sure. Old money. Nice for some."

I guess he hasn't heard what humans do to billionaires once they get sick of them. I look at that big, fancy house, and I wonder how much I could steal from it and actually get back to Earth. I bet he has some really nice things in there.

This is wild. I find myself on a distant alien estate and in the company of what appears to be landed alien gentry. Their weird, fancy, sprawling hyper-connected, almost neuronal city now seems like the artifice it is compared to this place, which is solid and timeless and real. Real the way a sunrise is, and the way an email is not.

SMACK

"OW!"

I let out a scream as Arkan's palm meets my ass in a hard slap. I should have expected that. He warned me. He more than warned me. I know I'm in a whole lot of trouble again — but I got distracted by the house. I thought I was better than to be impressed by material things, but there's something about an ancestral mansion that appeals to my DNA in ways I can't explain.

"You are going to be whipped and soaped until you beg for mercy," Arkan growls at me, thoroughly displeased, I think more with himself than with me. He must fancy himself quite the pet trainer. I am ruining his self-perception. If he is anything like most men, that's a sin far worse than biting.

Being carried and simultaneously spanked over the threshold of that alien mansion is something else. The foyer is elegantly carved with images of what I suppose must be Arkan's ancestors. I see images of animals that have no equal on Earth. Great beasts with fang and wing and claw, all rampant and fierce. It's the sort of decoration you get in a building where strength and power are valued.

I'd love to observe them more carefully, but a fire is being built in my rear that ignites the spanking he gave me before we left. I know other humans learn this way, but I refuse to learn from my mistakes. Every time his palm lands on my ass, a fresh bolt of heat and regret which I promptly deny rushes through me.

"You're a bad girl," he growls, his tone heavy with disapproval. "You've been very badly behaved, and that is over now. I will not tolerate any human disobedience. You may one day learn that there are rewards for being tame. There are also consequences for being wild."

We have now passed through the foyer and have entered whatever big fucking room you call the big fucking room beyond it. It's like Grand Central Station, but for a handful of aliens rather than an entire city. There are open door frames that lead into rooms off this main space, and a great, grand staircase that sweeps up the center and then wiggle-waggles in all directions. Sort of like a tree, I guess.

I'm having trouble taking this all in, because he's still spanking me very hard, and now he's going for my outfit, which is being torn from my body by his big, scaled hands. He is impatient with it, not bothering to find snaps or fasteners, simply yanking at it until it gives way and falls from my squirming body.

When he has me naked, he props one foot up on the lowest rung of the great many stairs and proceeds to put me over his thigh. My hips become a treacherous fulcrum and my ass is treated to a flurry of sharp slaps that make me wail for mercy I will not receive, and I would not accept.

The pain is beginning to intensify to new levels. I am aching, yet far from chastened. My skin stings. So does my pride.

"You are already bright red, on the verge of bruising, and still need so much punishing," he growls, his hand pressed against my rear.

I love hearing the frustration in his voice. This alien really thought he had me back there in the store. He thought I was so sorry, so broken, and all for a little soap and spanking. He knows better now.

There is an energy between us, a friction between human and alien, dominant force and unwilling submission. He can make me do what he wants, but that's not really what he wants. He wants me to want to do what he wants, and I won't give him that.

I feel his fingers shift, brushing lightly and perhaps even accidentally between my thighs. The seam of my lips tingles with the touch of his scaled alien fingertips.

He's supposed to be punishing me, but I suddenly don't feel punished anymore. I still feel sore, and small, but there is a welling of warmth and excitement between my legs and in the lowest parts of my belly. The pain that felt like it was becoming too much to bear suddenly becomes something else, a source of sexual energy.

"You are soaked," he says, pressing his fingertips more firmly against my sex, moving them in slow circles which makes the wetness between my lower lips spread even further.

It has been a long time since anybody touched me this way, and though I may hate what he has done to me in every sense, I cannot deny that I enjoy what he is doing now. The tension of my weeks of captivity is being greatly relieved by having my pussy played with.

"Do you enjoy punishment, pet?"

His question is low, growled, and rushes to the core of me. Yes. An inner voice cries out silently. *Yes, I love being punished.* It is a voice that surprises me to hear. I thought I hated punishment. I thought I hated him for daring to discipline me. But that was before he lit the tinder of my arousal.

The worst thing about this alien is how he makes me fight my own instincts. It's not just him I have to resist. It's everything in me, my every reaction, every need, every desire.

"I see," he says, as if he has heard me. I didn't say a word.

I know these aliens can read minds, but there has never been any indication that he could sense mine. Humans are supposed to be too simple and have nothing in the way of telepathic powers, but he just read my mind as if I were one of his own species.

"Do you want to be mated, pet?"

The question sinks through me and creates another rush of arousal which coats his fingers and makes the caressing of my pussy even more pleasurable. We are caught in a mutual feedback loop of desire, or at least I am. I don't know if he is just enjoying toying with me, treating me like a bad little pet, taking advantage of the arousal he has stoked in me.

I don't answer, not verbally, or mentally. I am too busy biting my lower lip and trying not to hump his thigh like a bitch in heat. He is making me feel like an animal with no self-control. I am being made to feel what he wants me to feel. His fingertips are spreading me now, parting my lower lips to expose the entrance to my body. One of his other fingers begins to probe, sliding into the tight entrance, pushing inside me, claiming me in a way no alien has ever dared claim me.

"Is this why you have been so impossible to tame? Are you in need of a good, hard mating?"

He asks the question as he buries his digit in my pussy. I feel my lips gripping his scaled finger, my hips arching back and forth, grinding my clit against the hard line of his alien leg. I am acting like an animal does, and I know it.

I want him.

He slides me off his lap and puts me on my knees on the steps of his big mansion. I look up the great stone vector, and I feel him part my thighs from behind. He is positioning me, getting me ready to be...

I want him inside me.

I want him to fuck me.

I want to feel him... I let out a moan as all my wants suddenly coalesce around the introduction of the thick head of an alien cock I cannot see but can absolutely feel the heat of, at the entrance of my pussy. I am wet. More than wet. I am soaked.

Ark's hand goes to the back of my neck, his fingers wrapping around my neck and reaching my throat. His grip is both powerful and intimate. I haven't answered his question, and it doesn't matter. We both know what I want, and what I need. I am kept in place quite easily as his massive form shifts carefully behind me and slides his cock right up inside my cunt.

He is big, designed to mate with a female of his species, but my pussy stretches for him, my inner walls parting to take him. I let out a helpless, happy little whimper. I have not been given a choice in the manner of my mating, but I do not care. He is making me feel like I belong to him, like I am not only his pet, but his true property.

My pussy is taut around his cock, my inner muscles clenching him with an absolute animal desperation. I want him inside me. I want him to keep me filled like this forever. I can't think. I can't do anything besides submit and be fucked by my alien owner.

For once, maybe for the first time since I met him, and probably long before, I relax. I let life happen. I let something greater than me fill me, pleasure me, and take care of me.

Arkan's lovemaking is passionate and intense and yes, with an edge of punitive intent. I am still in trouble. I am still his bad little pet. But I am also wrapped around his dick like the human fuck toy I am.

I feel my face pressed against ancient alien stone, my red hips rising beneath the dome of the roof as Arkan's cock spears deep inside me. He knows how to fuck, that's for sure. His hips grind and move to make his cock find every inch of me, the head of him repeatedly and near punishingly grinding across my g-spot.

This is not languid lovemaking. This is a fucking. This is designed to show me my place and claim me. He doesn't tell me this, he shows me in the rough and intense thrusting that takes us both rocketing toward climax.

"YES!" He growls the word in my ear, his hair falling in an intimate blue curtain around my head and shoulders as he arches his hips and pulls me back against his big, scaled, alien body.

Ark comes inside me, his seed filling me to the brim, some of it escaping even before his cock leaves me, the aching muscles of my sex no longer able to maintain their resistance. As he pulls out from me, I not only feel as though he has left, I feel like I have been physically emptied of a force I need.

I am left dripping with the evidence of our mating, of my defilement and my claiming. I am sore. My ass is sore, my pussy is sore, my pride is absolutely aching. How can I rebel now that he has shown me the true nature of what I actually desire?

I have not yet come. I wonder if he notices. I wonder if he cares.

Arkan scoops me up from the floor and proceeds to carry me up the stairs. This time he does not spank me the whole way. Instead, he cradles me close to his chest and rubs my rear with gentle and caring strokes. Occasionally his fingers stray close to my hungry yet ravaged sex, and I let out a little mewl of need.

"Bath time, pet," he murmurs as he takes me into a bath chamber which is made of more of that smooth stone. I feel myself squirm at the sight of it, remembering how it felt against my cheek when Arkan was deep inside me. I don't think I'm ever going to look at stone the same way again.

I find myself snuggling with him as he runs a bath the old fashioned way, then he gently places me into the very large, very luxurious tub and allows me to float happily in the relatively deep water. There was never enough water to bathe in on Earth. We'd wash ourselves with damp towels most of the time, because drinking water was very limited.

Oh no. It's happening. I'm starting to appreciate creature comforts. The post-coital feeling of wellbeing is suffusing me, taking away the tension that I'd usually have all the way in the pit of my stomach, leaving me blissfully floating in warm water.

I want to fight my own comfort, but it's just too comfortable. I figure it won't hurt to relax for a moment, right? I can let Arkan take care of me. Or failing that, I can at least take advantage of his bath.

"I should soap your mouth again for biting me again," he says, his tone slightly stern.

I let my hand drift down between my thighs, my fingertips finding my clit. He might not have let me come with his cock inside me, but he can't stop me from coming now.

"Uh uh," he corrects me, moving my hand away. "Orgasm is for good pets. Being fucked and used and left dripping cum, that is for the kind of pet you have decided to be."

I let out another sound of complaint, but privately I feel my pussy pulse with how goddamn hot his words are, coming to me in that alien growl through those wild and dangerous tusks. I'm supposed to feel punished, and I suppose I do, but it is hot as hell.

He starts washing my hair, using a cleansing lotion that smells like berries and yoghurt. The scent of it makes my stomach rumble as a new biological appetite comes rushing to the fore. I've lost weight on this alien world, too nervous to eat sometimes, and not being fed appropriately most of the rest. My owners used to feed me once a day according to their own appetites. These aliens only have one meal per day. It is a large one, but it works out to being one meal every couple of days if they make us eat on their schedule.

"You're hungry, aren't you," he says sympathetically. "I am sorry you have not been well taken care of since your arrival on this planet. I had hoped for better for you. I will ensure you have better from here on out."

"You can't stop other people from..."

"I can, because no other Euphorian will ever put hands on you again. I have decided to keep you for my own."

I turn in the bath to look at him. He gives me a tusk-ey smile as he rinses my hair.

"You were mine the moment I laid eyes on you. Your being sold was a mistake I tried to correct. You will not leave my side again, Jennifer. So you can stop fighting, and you need have no fear. You have found your alien master."

I try not to smile too wide. I fail.

4

When I wake, it is quiet. My belly is full and my body feels satisfied in spite of the fact I have been cruelly denied orgasm.

Arkan is asleep. I can hear the soft rhythmic sound of his breathing at the head of the bed. It is dark outside. Nights on Euphoria last almost twice as long as they do on Earth, as do days. This means humans get sleepy in the middle of the day and wake up in the middle of the night. Arkan has to know this about us, but I guess he figured I was super tired, enough to sleep through most of the Euphoric night.

Fortunately, the mechanisms on these crates are not really human-proof. The ones he uses for transport and in the shop are different. They are much more heavy-duty. But this one is a lighter home sort of edition and the metal on this bends in places if you know where to put pressure on. I know this because my previous owners tried to contain me in one of these.

The crate looks quite out of place in Ark's otherwise ornate and classically decorated bedroom. I was surprised when he dragged it out for me. I had assumed I would sleep in the bed with him, but he seems to think it is important I know my place — whatever that means.

It takes a little wrangling, but I manage to unclip the little latch that is supposed to keep me in. I've been very careful to never let the aliens see me do this.

While Arkan sleeps, I creep out of his bedroom on soft feet and make my way out into the hallway. This house is huge. Easily large enough to provide shelter for several families. The place I lived in back on Earth was so many times smaller than this I can't even put a mathematical number to it.

It seems perverse to me that one person would have so much space and so many riches. I haven't seen any poor aliens on Euphoria as yet, but experience tells me they have to exist.

I start going from room to room. Most of the rooms up here are bedrooms, and they're all empty. Coming from a planet with a perpetual housing crisis, it's like a slap in the face to go from room to room and find nothing but fancy big beds and even fancier decorations.

The impulse to make this stuff mine is too much to bear. I start snatching things here and there, just the shiny things, the gold and the silver and anything that gleams. I'm not entirely sure what I'm going to do with them. I guess I'll stash them somewhere so I can get them on the spaceship I intend to steal.

If I'm honest, I've gotten distracted. Ripping Arkan's ancestral home off has become a means to its own end. I know he's not one of the people who fucked the rest of the planet over back on Earth, but stealing his stuff is like a symbolic victory.

I use a bed sheet to gather everything together as I take enough stuff to not be able to hold it all in my hands. I know I can't take everything I want, but I want to take as much as I can.

This isn't the way he probably intended his night to end. He probably thinks fucking me and feeding me means I'm dedicated to him, but I am a survivor and I know that at the end of the day the only creature I can ever be dedicated to is myself. As hot as he is, I can't trust him. I can only trust myself.

Having moved through many of the upper bedrooms, I start to get hungry again. It's work, carrying an increasingly expanding collection of stolen material. I decide to abscond from the higher reaches of this mansion and get back down to the kitchen.

Carefully padding down the stairs with a bedsheet full of fine treasures hoisted over my shoulder, I am thrilled with my subversive actions. Sure, I'm ripping off the alien I just had sex with for the first time, but if I'm honest — and I rarely am, that kind of adds to the thrill. I might be stealing some of his things, but he already stole the actual all of me.

He deserves this, I tell myself. They all deserve this. If I could get a shuttle and work out how to fly it, I could go around ripping off all these aliens and then take my ill-gotten gains back to Earth. Or maybe I could retreat into the big wild forests I've seen from the grate of my travel crate, and start a civilization of rebel humans living a human life on this planet.

There are so many possibilities, and with all these riches I am convinced that I can make a new life for myself wherever I choose. These are not just things. These are the harbingers of freedom.

"What are you doing, human?"

Arkan's voice booms from in front of me, giving me a hell of a fright. I drop my sack of stolen goods, which promptly rolls down at least a hundred stairs, shedding bits of pretty tat everywhere in an uproarious cacophony of metal on stone.

I follow them, slipping on the falling sheet somehow and becoming another object sliding down the stairs on an impromptu raft of cloth and shame, bumping each and every step on my way down with my already sore rear.

Before I can break my neck, I am scooped up mid-fall by strong arms, and I look up into strange eyes.

"Who the fuck are you?" I blurt the question.

It's not Arkan. It's someone who looks like him, and sounds like him, but isn't him, and doesn't know me. His hair is blue, but it is much shorter than Ark's. It ends around his shoulders, whereas Ark's is almost all the way down his back.

"You're lucky you didn't kill yourself!" he exclaims, deeply unimpressed.

He speaks fluent English as well. A twin? A brother? Arkan hasn't spoken about his family. Arkan hasn't spoken about a lot of things. My mind slips back to the banquet debacle with Melinda. Is this Kahn?

This new guy gives me a shake, as if he is expecting an answer. My mind is working far more slowly than it should. I suddenly realize that I have met him before, sort of. He was the one who told the family to take the crate I am in. He sold me without bothering to look at me. He sold me like I was a fucking box of soda. That does mean he has absolutely no idea who I am.

I don't want to say a word. Whoever this guy is, and however much he might look like Arkan, he doesn't have Arkan's softer edges. I can feel that already. This brother has a similar appearance, but a totally different energy to Ark.

"Breaking into our home, stealing our goods. What would you have done with them?"

I don't answer. I have to hope that Arkan will hear this commotion and come down and save me from this doppelgänger. Falling down the stairs with a sheet full of stolen metal items wasn't exactly a quiet affair.

"No answer? Very well. Let me see if I can loosen your tongue."

He props his foot up on the stairs and I already know what is going to happen. He's right about this making me break my silence.

"No!" I shriek the word as he turns me over his knee. "I've had two spankings in one day! I can't take a third!"

"The first two clearly didn't work."

His palm meets my ass hard, and I shriek not just in pain, but in panic.

"ARK!" I yell for the alien who abducted me. "I'M BEING KILLED!"

Finally, Arkan makes an appearance, though not before Kahn gives me a good ten slaps right to the seat of my nightgown-covered ass. Every single one of them hits home, sending jolts of harsh heat rushing through me. I wail and thrash around in the attempt to escape, but Kahn has me in a tight grip.

"Kahn," Arkan says, appearing at the top of the stairs. He looks sleepy and confused to find me in his brother's grasp. "What's going on?"

"I thought we agreed, no pets at home," Kahn says, keeping his grip on me. "Especially thieving little animals like this one."

"What are you..." Arkan looks around and sees the various knick-knacks and accoutrements of various bedrooms now strewn about the base of the stairs. He comes down the stairs clad in his alien pajamas, a shining robe wrapped around his body. His feet are bare. He stops where the sheet has been left, runs his hand through his long hair with a perplexed expression, and stares at me.

"What did you do, pet?"

"Nothing," I lie.

The lie is accompanied by another fiendishly hard slap that makes me yowl.

"How are you out of your crate?" Arkan scowls at me.

"He's beating me!" I wail plaintively. "Help!"

"You'll get a proper whipping if you don't start answering our questions," Kahn lectures me. His voice is slightly rougher than Arkan's, but he's not quite as large in stature. Still, even being smaller than Arkan means nothing when he has the grip strength of an extraterrestrial primate.

I do not want to answer questions, but the price of silence appears to be pain, and I truly cannot take another one of those harsh alien slaps. I thought it was bad enough to be punished by Arkan. It is a thousand times worse to be punished in front of him by a complete stranger who regards me as nothing more than a common thief deserving of a thrashing.

I hesitate again, and once more I am punished with a sharp slap to my rear that makes me yowl like an actual animal. Kahn has me propped over his thigh, in a similar way to the fashion Arkan punished me earlier, in pretty much the same place. This is like a very painful deja-vu. All roads seem to lead to being put over alien laps and spanked. Why must I suffer this misfortune? What have I done so wrong? It seems all very unfair.

Arkan steps down a few more steps to stand in front of me. He takes my chin in his hand and directs my rebellious, self-pitying gaze to his handsome, befanged face.

"How did you get out of your crate, and what were you doing with all of these trinkets?"

Looking into his eyes while being held firm over his brother's lap, I find myself melting into something close enough to obedience to allow myself to reply.

"Your crates suck," I tell him. "And I was taking all this stuff because you took me. So you owe me. I was going to make, like, a planetary escape fund with it."

There is a moment of silence in which I brace myself for a lot more pain. Surely I am going to feel an absolute thunder of slaps on my already over-punished ass.

Instead, there is a snort. A snort followed by a chuckle, and then a full peal of laughter. They are both laughing, Kahn and Arkan. I feel Kahn's powerful body making me vibrate with the force of his amusement, my crotch pressed firmly and with a slight ache against his hard thigh. This is an indecent situation made no better by mirth.

"What the fuck are you laughing at?"

"Language, pet," Arkan says.

"Respect, pet," Kahn says at practically the same time.

My problems have just doubled. I am in an entirely new kind of trouble now. Escaping Arkan's attentions was one thing, but now with his brother here it seems as though there's no way to escape. Mostly because his brother still has me firmly in hand.

"Humans," Kahn says in what sounds like long suffering terms. "This is why we don't have pets at home."

There's silence in response, which means they've gone into their alien speak. They're talking about me and I can't hear it, which is very weird and inconvenient given I am stuck here over Kahn's thigh with my rear burning in the most uncomfortable of ways.

"Where were you going next?" Arkan asks the question with a kind of stern indulgence. "Once you had your escape fund secured?"

"To get some food. I'm hungry."

"Alright," he sighs. "Let's feed you. And then I'm putting you back in your crate, and you are going to stay there if you have any sense of what is good for you. Tomorrow, you show me how you escaped."

"Sure, if I can remember."

"You'll remember, or you will be sore."

I am already sore, which means I have little more to fear, but I don't say that. I know when to keep my mouth shut sometimes.

"You can let her go, Kahn," Arkan says.

There's another brief exchange of private telepathic talk before Kahn sighs and lets me wriggle free of his grip and thigh. I am glad for the modesty of my nightgown, and for the fact that when I tilt my head forward, my hair falls over my face and I don't have to look at either of the tall, tusked aliens who are looming over me with disapproving vibes.

It's hellishly embarrassing to be caught stealing this way. I feel like a complete amateur. Worse, I feel small, and human, and not in a good way. I've done my best to never let myself think of these aliens as being any better than me. So what if they're shiny, massive, telepathic geniuses with a world that actually functions socially and environmentally? I'm from Earth, and that should mean something.

"Come," Arkan says, reaching for my hand and taking it in his much bigger palm. He wants me under control, no further away from him than his arm can go. I'm glad for him to have my hand if it means Kahn's hand isn't on my ass anymore.

"Pancakes?" Arkan asks me the question as we get to the kitchen. I am flooded with anticipation and goodwill. The prospect of hot, buttery pancakes made just the way they'd be made on Earth almost makes me cry. I think I might love him.

"You should make her something simple. Warm grains. After her behavior, she does not deserve to enjoy food."

Kahn has followed us, which is annoying given how large the house is. Surely he has somewhere else to be and something else to do.

"The fuck is your problem?" I turn to face Kahn, annoyed and disrespectful.

"Enough, pet," Arkan says.

Kahn gives me a death stare and looks as though he wants to come over the table at me. Arkan moves slightly, as if to prevent such an action, should it occur.

"A pet should be taught her place," he insists. I know he's saying it to get a rise out of me, because he could be saying this telepathically to Arkan, and he's not. He's making sure I hear every word.

Fortunately, Arkan is going about the business of making pancakes, so I know that Kahn's backseat cooking is not having any real effect on him.

I take a fork from the cutlery drawer and give Kahn a look over the tines. I don't know why he's still hanging about.

I can tell they're arguing in their heads again. I wonder what Kahn is saying. Arkan seems largely impassive, unbothered by Kahn's obvious judgement. I'm leaning against the kitchen counter. I couldn't sit if I wanted to. My ass is absolutely burning. I'm not going to sit for days, probably. But the physical discomfort is nothing on the shame I feel with Kahn's eyes on me. He's a stranger, an arrogant, cocky, dominant asshole and he thinks he has the right to put his hands on me and punish me even though I don't belong to him.

I belong to Arkan.

I mean, I don't belong to anybody, because I am a human and humans cannot be owned. I have to remind myself of that very consciously because my ass is not the only part of me that is aching. I can still feel the effects of Arkan's mating, and I will never forget it. He said he'd claimed me, and I think that might be true. Sure, I was going to rip him off and run away, but that's neither here nor there. Arkan has more claim to me than Kahn does, that's for certain.

The smell of butter in a hot pan immediately improves my mood. Arkan is already starting to whip up a batter. In a matter of minutes, I'll be feasting on fresh pancakes, and nothing Kahn says will matter. I grip my fork more tightly, refusing to let him ruin the meal. I spent too long hungry to waste opportunities to eat.

"Let her eat, Kahn," Arkan says calmly.

"I'm not stopping her eating. I'm telling you that this is no place for spoiled little returned pets. I'm telling you..." He goes silent again, but the tension in his face, especially around his jaw tells me that he's not pleased. His tusks are gleaming as if they yearn to rend flesh.

Arkan slides the first pancake onto my plate, and I start eating. It's very good. Rich and buttery, and also light and fluffy. I'm immediately in absolute heaven, no longer caring about anything I've done, or suffered. I'll take three more beatings for one more of these pancakes.

5

Arkan

Once we have my pet safely secured inside the crate once more, and inside a well-locked room, Kahn and I pick up all the stolen pieces of decor and return them to their proper places. It is quite an onerous task. She really was quite thorough as she rifled through the treasures and keepsakes of our ancestral home.

"You should have made her do this," Kahn complains.

"She needs rest."

"Soft," Kahn grunts with distaste.

I do not care what my younger brother thinks about how I handle my human. She is not his problem, and he certainly has no authority over me.

Having restored our home, we retreat for drinks. I know he's not really angry about the human. He has his own problems to worry about, but he'd prefer to grumble about my pet than focus on them.

"We did agree no pets." Kahn reminds me of the rule that I myself made.

"I know, but this one was on the verge of being destroyed. I had to do something."

"Could have left her at the shop."

"Turns out, I couldn't. Imagine if she had broken out there. We might never have found her. She's the one you sold without checking, Kahn. You played a role in this mess, so you might want to let the righteous act drop."

Kahn does not let the righteous act drop. Not even a little bit.

"It's not like you to select a human who wouldn't make a suitable pet," Kahn says. "And that human has close to no signs of being a suitable pet. She's not submissive. She's not sweet. She has criminal tendencies. She..."

I take a long swig of fermented fruit beverage as Kahn lists the many obvious shortcomings of my human pet. He's not wrong about a single thing. She has a wild temperament, and she is clearly given to criminality, but those are survival traits, and I very much admire them. Kahn does not agree. Kahn expects obedience almost before a pet is tamed.

"How did the meeting go?" I ask.

I don't really need to know the answer to that question. It is obvious that the meeting Kahn had with the Euphorian council went poorly.

"They want to open up the permit process. Wrathelders have been petitioning them. They say it is unfair that our family has a monopoly on the human pet trade. I told them selection matters, and that bringing just one or two of the wrong humans here could quite literally destroy our civilization, but they didn't believe me. I could tell they thought we just want to keep competition out of the industry. If Euphoria is filled with enough breeding humans, they could easily form wild pockets and create a hostile civilization right under the noses of these idiots who sit in their pale towers and make decrees about things they do not begin to understand. Look what humans did to their own planet! How can anybody think they would be any kinder to ours?"

I listen as he rants aloud, using a more primal form of communication to express his frustration. No wonder he was so furious when he found my pet loose in the house after a day like the one he has had. Kahn respects humans more than most of our kind. He understands that they can be genuinely dangerous.

"There are humans who would understand our technology and even devise ways to use them against us. I tried to warn the council, but they don't believe it to be a problem. They're looking at the numbers, and at the demand. Wrathelders are pushing for more in-home breeding too. We have such a limited pool of humans here, and they want to start cross-breeding. It's madness. Imagine how related some of them already are, and how interrelated they will be after just a few generations..."

Kahn is smart, resourceful, and powerful. He suffers greatly because others are not as smart or forward thinking, and he spends much of his life trying to explain consequences to others. It is a source of perpetual torment.

"We need limits on human populations, and we need bans on breeding. It is easy enough to render the males sterile without impinging on their physical health. Even on Earth, vasectomies were practiced regularly."

He is not talking to me so much as expounding on the very same points he would have spent all day trying to make to no avail. Another powerful family, the Wrathelders, are lobbying to transport humans, and in far greater numbers, and at much lower rates.

I have not greatly concerned myself with these matters. Kahn likes to deal with officials. I prefer to focus on the humans we are training and saving. But there comes a time when ignoring matters of state is no longer an option, and it seems as though that time is upon me.

"At the meeting, Phenix Wrathelder unveiled a design for a ship that could take upwards of ten thousand humans in a single trip. I told him that would be ecological suicide. Do you know what he said?"

"No."

"He said that if some of them do get free, they would be amusing to hunt." Kahn looks at me with an expression of restrained horror. "We're trying to preserve the human species. That's what the license is supposed to do. But the whole exercise is in the proceeds of being corrupted by greed. It sickens me."

The Wrathelders are not to be dismissed lightly. They had little interest in our human pet project to begin with. It sounded far too much like charity and conservation for their liking. But as the popularity of human pets grew, and the profits became more obvious, it was inevitable they would begin to take interest.

"You know they have weight with the council," Kahn says. "It's only a matter of time before they're bringing in shipments of humans without any selection criteria or training. They'll be wild. They'll be destructive. They'll be riddled with disease and parasites. The males will form defensive bands, and the females will become pregnant and distressed at the loss of their mates. There is every chance they will bring young to the planet too. They won't have our restraint or protocols about not separating mothers from young. It will be a tragedy."

I am listening, silently mentally agreeing to everything he is saying. In the very old days, our family, the Voros, would have approached the Wrathelders and negotiated a way out of this situation. In more modern times, few are open to such negotiation. The Wrathelders and the Voros have staked their claims and bad blood has been allowed to fester between us.

"Maybe what we need to do is show the council what a wild human is really like," I suggest. "It just so happens we have a completely uncontrolled little specimen upstairs. When I tell you what she did to her first owners, you'll be very much displeased. But we could always..."

"Unleash her on the council, with her rabid appetite for pancakes and disrespect?"

Kahn is not immediately convinced, though a slight smile does appear on his features.

"It would be amusing," he admits. "If nothing else. But it may also prove that we have no control over our human pets, and the Wrathelders may as well have a permit to import as well."

"We already look like we are importing wild humans. Jennifer spent three days absolutely terrorizing everybody she met until her owners returned her."

His expression becomes solemn again. "I am sorry I sold her. You are right. I should have been much more careful. Things have been so much busier now that it is just the two of us."

There are four of us brothers, but only Kahn and I are of any use these days.

"Don't worry. I should have made certain you knew what I was doing with her. It would be nice if Rake would at least come back and help."

"Rake," Kahn sighs. "Where is our little brother?"

"Back in the woods, I assume."

Rake is younger than Kahn by three minutes and is the embodiment of wildness and chaos. He's the complete opposite of Kahn in terms of temperament. Usually, I do not mind his uncivilized ways, but it does cause problems when he appears from wherever he's been to throw as many wrenches in as many gears as possible before sinking back beneath the waters of his own personal chaos. Personally, I think we are probably slightly better off without our younger siblings.

Between Kahn's obsessive need for order, and Rake's refusal of it, I'm the middle man. The oldest brother. The one who has to bring calm to what might otherwise be the incendiary relationships of our band of brothers.

"If father were here..." Kahn begins.

"Father is not here. We are. We will deal with this. Don't worry."

"I am worried. The Wrathelders have been gaining power steadily, courting influence, gaining allies and enemies who cannot refuse them. We have been playing intergalactic pet shop while they build an empire." Kahn looks at me reproachfully.

His silent judgement, given without word or thought, reaches me regardless. I am not the politician our father was. I'm also not dead like he is either. There are prices to be paid for seeking political power, and death is one of them. We may appear to be a peaceful, civilized species, but behind the facade of telepathic propriety, we are as treacherous and dangerous as any animal in any wild place in the universe.

"Do not worry. They have never prevailed, and they will never prevail. Even when they killed father, they did not gain anything from it."

"They took Zain's freedom."

"Zain took Zain's freedom. We told him not to seek vengeance."

"We should visit him again. He's due another care package."

Our youngest brother is serving a life sentence in prison for the attempted murder of Phenix Wrathelder. In the wake of our father's death, he decided to take justice into his own hands. It did not go well. To this day, there is no evidence that Phenix Wrathelder was truly responsible for our father's assassination, but Zain remains convinced of Phenix's guilt. Privately, so are we all.

"We should," I agree.

It has been nearly three years since Zain was put behind bars. We have exhausted legal means to extract him, in large part because he is no help to himself. Every report from the prison commissar's desk details fighting and other minor crimes that would extend his sentence if his sentence was not already for life.

Holding a family of brothers together is no easy task. I prefer wrangling humans. Even the worst behaved among them is relatively easy to handle compared to my strong-willed siblings.

Kahn drains his drink. "I'm going to bed," he says. "If I encounter that human of yours again, I'm going to whip her until she cries. She's absolutely undisciplined, and a complete liability."

I give him a steady look. I want him to very much internalize the meaning of my next words.

"She's mine."

"What is that supposed to mean?"

He knows what it means, but I elaborate so there is absolutely no confusion going forward.

"I mean she's *mine*. I understand why you punished her when you first met her. You didn't know who she was, or why she was here. You were punishing a thief. But she is mine to train."

"Then keep her out of my way."

I narrow my eyes slightly and consider what I am going to do with Kahn. He is so sensitive to disrespect from those he considers to be lesser beings, but he doesn't seem to notice his own ample amounts of disrespect which he doles out without any concern.

I know he believes he is the most responsible and functional of us all in spite of being second born. He takes on responsibilities in a near compulsive way, imagining that if he can only have control of things, they will never go wrong. Our father's passing only made that innate tendency worse. But I am the head of this family, and though I rarely insist upon his submission to my will, when it comes to my pet, I will not tolerate him touching her again.

"I mean..." Kahn clears his throat when he sees my expression. "I mean..."

A single look can get someone to change their tune when they know what potentially lurks behind that expression.

"You should get some rest," I say cooly.

"I should," he agrees. "Goodnight."

"Night."

I let Kahn make his escape from my presence without further pushing the issue of respect. He knows what is good for him, and the ice in my verbal and mental tone alone should have told him to stay well clear of my pet from now on.

Kahn leaves for bed, but I stay in the drinking room for a short while. I am too alert to sleep now, or perhaps simply too concerned. Speaking with Kahn reminds me of the many complexities of this world, of the ties I was born into, the innumerable responsibilities that fall on my shoulders. I think about Zain, and how long it has been since I saw him. At first I refused to visit. I was so angry at him for the failed attempt that only saw him put behind bars. Perhaps something has softened inside me. I feel the need to go and see him.

It has been too long, and I have been avoiding him. In the wake of my father's passing, all of us have found our own ways to avoid the pain. Zain is in prison, Rake is in the wilderness, Kahn has become a bureaucratic warrior, and I have thrown myself into all things human.

If the Wrathelders are on the rise, it is time to regather. We have spent years grieving. Now we need to find our strength to save humans and the future of Euphoria itself.

It's all very inspiring. I'm not entirely sure I'd be so cheerful at the prospect of facing our oldest familial enemies if it wasn't for the fact that my time with my pet has put me in a very, very good mood. Having mated with her even once, I feel as though I could face any obstacle. As weak as my human mate is in the physical sense, she makes me strong. She makes me determined to ensure that the future of her kind is bright.

I'm sure Kahn wouldn't approve if he knew what else I'd done with my human pet. I have never mated a human before. We do not sell our pets with the understanding they will be used for base fornication, though of course, from time to time, there are rumors of mating, and even infidelities in which some Euphorian males have chosen human mates over their own bonded mates. Quite scandalous, and usually looked upon with great derision — especially by the female mates concerned.

My brothers and I remain single, long after the age most men of our species mate and marry. I have always figured it was because of the unfortunate circumstances of our parents' union. My father is dead. My mother... I cannot bear to think of what became of her.

Our once proud family was shattered by my father's death and my mother's... there are so many words for what she did to us, and none of them are pleasant. Even the worst behaved human feels more predictable and safe than a Euphorian female now.

There have been many pretty humans passing through the doors of our pet shop, but it is not Jennifer's appearance that made my lust so powerfully insatiable I could not resist. It is her spirit. She has as much fire in her as any Euphorian. She is strong in ways I find myself admiring even as it brings great chaos to my world.

Finally, fatigue begins to creep back into my body. It is very late and my sleep has been disturbed by my pet's little criminal excursion, but I am glad for it. I needed to hear Kahn's news. I had barely remembered that he was at the council today, far too obsessed with my own problems and then the charming charisma of my human pet, who makes all other concerns seem like matters of no note whatsoever.

Is this love? When one is concerned and unconcerned, free and shackled, all at the same time? Where nothing matters at all, and yet everything is tremendously important because it must be perfect for her? I do not know. I have never felt love toward a mate before. I have felt desire, and a certain biological relief once that desire was physically relieved, but nothing like this, not a warmth of feeling and deep affection that not only persists but seems to intensify with each passing moment post coitus.

I feel a pull of yearning that compels me to drain the dregs of my beverage and rise to my feet. I miss my pet.

The crate door is open when I get back to the bedroom. I glance down, though I do not really need to. I already know that my pet is not in her crate. For a moment, I fear I have been terribly foolish and allowed her to escape, but a second later I spot her curled up quite happily in my bed. She has clearly decided she is too good for her crate and prefers a proper bed for her repose.

She is fast asleep.

The trainer in me says I should put her back in her crate, but instead I very carefully lift the covers and slide in next to her. She is small but warm, and there is a comfort to her presence that soon has me sliding into slumber alongside her.

6

J*en*

I wake up curled up next to a big, warm alien. My ass is aching, and so is my pussy. I feel as though I have been run over by a big, sexy truck. I also feel very snuggly and very comfortable, and... Happy? Yes. I feel happy. It's a strange, light sensation that makes me squirm a little against Ark's body, feeling the hard, long lines of his sleeping form.

I should be escaping. It's the perfect time. He's not even awake. I could tip-toe on out of here and, hopefully avoiding his asshole brother, be the closest thing to free I've been in some time.

But the bed is warm and the blankets are extra snuggly and instead I close my eyes again and let myself go back to sleep.

I wake up for a second time to the smell of fresh cooking. When I open my eyes, I am no longer accompanied in the bed. I am alone in the sheets, but Ark is beside me with a tray of food. More pancakes, and a citrus type drink.

"You made me breakfast?" I can't keep the surprise and gratitude out of my voice.

"I know humans need to eat regularly," he says. "You need to keep your strength up."

He's trying to sound like he's being logical about this, but I know a romantic gesture when I see it. Especially when he puts the tray down over my legs and I see that there's a little flower on the side of the plate. Nothing too flashy, just a little white and yellow daisy type flower, but certainly nothing that needs to be there.

The tray and everything on it suddenly seems very misty for some reason, as if I am looking through a blurry filter. I blink and realize that there are tears in my eyes. Happy tears. How weird.

"What's wrong?" Ark seems immediately concerned.

I look up at him. He's blurry, but hot and handsome in spite of his blurriness. "Nothing's wrong," I say, my voice quavering. "It's just, you're making it very hard to want to run away."

"Good," he smiles, reaching out to caress my hair. "I want you to stay with me, pet. I want to take good care of you. I want to make you happy."

I groan inwardly. I've sworn to make him regret ever having taken me from Earth, and this sweetness is fully ruining that plan of mine.

I take a bite of the pancakes before they get cold. They're good again, just like they were last night. I wonder if he's going to give me pancakes for every meal. I could live with it if he was.

"They're very good," I say, answering the question I can see hovering on his face.

"Good," he says. "I used a fortified flour to ensure they have additional nutritional value. I also added a protein powder, as you have not consumed much of the way in protein lately."

He sits on the bed, his scaled arms rippling casually as he slides them back to prop himself up. His hair is tied back behind his head in a ponytail, and he is wearing the closest thing I have seen any of these aliens wear to a suit.

It is a stiff, formal garment with trousers and a jacket, though he does not wear any shirt beneath it.

"What are you so dressed up for?"

"I may later regret this, but I have matters of importance to deal with today. I could leave you in a secure location, but I am not certain that any location is secure where you are concerned. I am curious. How did you support yourself on Earth?"

"A little of this, a little of that." My reply is evasive because I've learned over time not to incriminate myself. It's not as if I can be punished for what I did back there. Right? Right. Or maybe? Hard to say. Definitely easier not to say.

Ark gives me a stern stare through golden eyes. "I am not trying to trick you into confessing past crimes," he says. "But I do find it interesting how quickly you were able to break out of your crate."

"It's just not a very good crate," I explain with a grin that I cannot help because I know that answer drives him fucking mad. It's one little piece of control I have in a world and existence that feels very much entirely out of my control.

"Obviously you were able to manipulate the latch."

"Obviously."

I cannot get the shit-eating grin off my face. The harder he stares at me, the funnier I find this.

"You have some talent for escape and for evasion, pet," he says. "I can see that. I'm simply curious where it came from."

His question sends my mind cartwheeling back to darker times and worse places. I don't like thinking about Earth. I yearn for it because it is home, but when I think about specifics, I feel a certain dark curtain falling around me. Life was not easy before I was taken.

"Let's just say it was a skill borne out of necessity and leave it at that, shall we?"

Ark crouches down next to me, taking one knee next to the bed, his golden gaze on a level with mine.

"I want to know, pet. I want to know everything about you."

Something inside me wants to break and tell him my whole sorry, sordid story. But there are stronger impulses. Like the one to shut up and protect myself.

"There's not much to tell," I lie with a little shrug.

"I will hear your stories one day, pet," he says. "But for today, I need you to resist any temptation you have to run. I have serious business to attend to, and I am going to have you with me. You will wear a collar, and a leash, and you will behave yourself."

I start to grin again as he tells me I will behave, but his eyes narrow and his features sharpen with a certain kind of intensity that tells me I don't want to fuck around.

I have been punished multiple times in the last twenty-four hours. I am ready to take a break from being in trouble.

"Okay," I agree. "But only because you made me pancakes."

"Good. I'll take your good behavior for any reason at this point," he says, standing up. "Stay there," he says. "I have something for you."

The *something for me* turns out to be a blue silk dress in fabric very much like the fabric his own attire is made of. We are going to be matchy-matchy, and suddenly I am very much here for it.

The bodice fits nicely, and the skirt comes down to just above my knees. It looks like a proper piece of clothing, not some animal costume. With matching boots with gold laces that run all the way up to my knees, I feel comfortable and stylish and only slightly like a professional wrestler slash anime girl.

I stand before the mirror in his room, turning back and forth to see how the skirt flares with my motion. It doesn't just look good, it fits me perfectly. I have curves. I have a big ass. Usually skirts that fit in the chest and waist cling to my rear like an anaconda attempting to devour a sheep. But this is cut to fit my pear shape as if the maker had studied my body for years.

"You had this outfit all ready to go?"

He pauses for a moment, as if considering whether or not to confess something to me.

"I had this made after I captured you, and before you were sold."

I frown a little. "Does that mean you were intending on keeping me?"

He nods. "Yes. But my brother was not aware, and so you were sold, and once sold, I thought you might find a happy home with your new owners."

"That didn't happen, obviously," I point out bluntly.

"No," he smiles. "It did not. I should have retrieved you immediately in hindsight, but that is a mistake that will stay in the past. I will certainly never let you go again."

Those last words make me freeze with an odd kind of hope. "You won't? You're not going to sell me again, once I'm good?"

"No," he says, picking up a hairbrush. I feel my ass get hot at the sight of it, but it is not intended for my rear. Instead he gestures for me to take a seat and starts to brush my hair. I sit on the bed and let him tend to me, enjoying the feeling of bristles running over my scalp.

It seems there are certain advantages to being good. Ark certainly seems to like me, which surprises me given how awful I've been from the moment I met him until around about now. I had my reasons, of course. I was scared, I was angry, I was fucking sold. I've been struggling for survival on this planet in a different way than I used to struggle on Earth. There, it was holding my body together that was the problem. Here it feels like my mind is what is at stake, keeping myself a free creature in spite of all the pressure to collapse internally.

"Today may be challenging for you. It will certainly be challenging for me. I ask that you restrain any impulses to chaos, not because the consequence will be punishment, but because I am asking nicely."

"Appealing to my better nature. That's a risky approach."

Ark snorts gently. "I am sure it is."

With my hair brushed out into silky skeins, he brushes it back from my face and brings another item to bear, a light but colorful collar that flashes pink and red for a second before turning gold and blue to match the outfit. A leash follows, clipped to the collar and then attached to his belt. I now have approximately four feet of free movement.

"Don't scowl," Ark chides me gently. "It is not so bad."

"No? You put the fucking collar on then, and I'll hold the leash."

He chuckles. "You don't need to worry about me running away and doing something dangerous. This is for your safety."

I'm not going to argue. I know he is treating me well. He's being very nice to me, and he doesn't have to be. He could do what my previous owners did and lock me away until I thought I was going to go completely mad. I have honed my escape skills on this planet out of mental health necessity.

"Ready to go, I think," Ark says, brushing my hair away from my face again. "You look very sweet, pet."

"Then this isn't an outfit. It's a disguise."

We travel into the city, and not in his pet moving truck, but in one of the sleek flying saucer type vehicles that skim about the place day and night. I remember when humans thought they were going to get flying machines like this. Never actually eventuated. Not even for very rich people, which was a bit of a surprise.

Ark pilots toward the very center of the city, where the spire-topped buildings are at their highest, and the spiderweb tendrils of footpaths are at their densest. Sitting beside him in the bulbous transparent cab of the machine, I feel perfectly safe, which is wild considering we are hurtling through the air at incredible speeds.

At the very center of the city is a building that I assume has to be their government building. It has a certain dark gravitas to it. Unlike most of the buildings which are a pale sandstone to pearl white in hue, this one is obsidian black and stands imposingly at the very center of it all. From the height of Ark's ship, the city looks like a wheel or an eye. Everything emanates from this dark center.

Ark dips the controls and we begin to spiral down around the dark concrescence, going far lower than most of the other spire buildings, down to the shadows of the cluster of buildings until we land on a heavily guarded platform replete with sentries holding very imposing looking weapons.

I'm surprised when Ark slides the hood of the vehicle open and steps out, motioning for me to follow. Nobody so much as asks him who he is, which means they must know who he is. This doesn't seem like the sort of place people just wander in and out of.

I press much closer to him than my leash requires. I do not like this place. It feels oppressive and heavy. Most of the city is just your general decadent futuristic utopia, but there is a pall over this part of it, a place where the sun never shines.

"What is this place?" I whisper the question to Ark while I feel the eyes of the guards on me. These guys have a very different vibe to the cake indulging aristocrats I am used to. They are broader, more powerful, and not one of them looks like they eat cake. They ripple under tight uniforms that show off scales and muscles alike.

"It is a prison," Ark says.

I look at him with wide eyes. Did I piss him off that much by trying to steal all his many items last night? Is he done with me? Is this where all the very worst pets go?

"But... I thought you were going to keep me?"

"You're not going to prison," Ark chuckles, thoroughly amused. "My brother is here."

"He's a prison warden? Makes sense. Seems like something your family would be into."

He does not reply. Instead, he looks solemn and perhaps a little hurt. I shut up about three sentences too late and follow him into the interior of this dark palace, through a door grilled with lasers that scan us both as we pass through. I have no choice. My leash is firmly attached to his belt. Where he goes, I go.

"Arkan Voros to see Zain Voros," he says to the stern looking guard who greets us once the heavy bars have closed behind us, swallowing us into the interior of the prison.

I am beginning to find it hard to breathe easily. My chest feels tight. My head feels light. The walls themselves seem to be sliding toward me.

I have been in a place like this before. I have been cut off from the light and from my freedom. It was a place like this that made me yearn for open spaces and making my own way no matter what.

Ark is moving deeper into the prison, through stony passages marked intermittently with bars that lead to cages of the kind even I could not get out of. The oppression in this place is so intense and so deep it sinks into my very bones. I take a deep breath to try to calm myself. It is only partially successful, air hitching and catching in my throat.

"Zain is in solitary for attacks on the guards. He'll not have any visitors today." A large, green-tinged guard with very sharp lower tusks materializes suddenly in our path.

"I have not seen my brother in months," Ark replies. "It is imperative I see him today, and illegal for you to withhold my access. As head of my family, I am entitled to inspect his conditions four times per year."

The guard grunts, not liking the fact that Ark appears to know his rights.

"The animal can't come."

"She's my possession and she will come," Ark replies calmly. "Please escort me to my brother at once. I do not have time to quibble over irrelevant details."

I suddenly realize who he is channeling. He sounds like his brother, Kahn. He has the same officious and stern tone. It's very effective. The guard, as high ranking as he seems to be, folds like a paper airplane, and we get the dubious pleasure of going ever deeper into the prison.

Ark

I feel my pet pressing close to me as we descend into the bowels of the Deep. This is a miserable place, and I feel somewhat guilty for bringing her here. She seems scared, and I cannot blame her.

Reaching out to put my hand on her back to calm her, I find that her presence calms me too. It has been a long time since I had someone I liked by my side. Someone I trust, too, though she has not done much to earn that trust. I know she will run if she can. I know she will disobey me to every extent I allow it, and yet there is a part of me that finds her eminently trustworthy.

Because she is your mate, my inner voice says. *She is the one who was made for you in the beginning. She is your destiny.*

According to the customs of our people, only another Euphorian can be my mate. A tall, statuesque creature of my own kind. That is who should be my mate. Not this chaotic little human who came to my world as a commodity.

You do not understand fate. There are events and consequences and forces at play far beyond your limited understanding of what is.

My inner voice is sometimes kind of an asshole, but I've overheard other people's internal voices, and relatively speaking mine is only pedantic and whimsical, which I will take over the harsh cruelty some of my kind must tolerate inside their skulls.

An elevator takes us several thousand feet below the surface of the planet, to a dungeon more ancient than almost any other structure we have. The black spire building above is built over the ruins of the castle of our first royal family. Some say the land is cursed, but it does not matter. It is the vortex at the core of our civilization, necessary because one cannot have dark without light.

"They told me my brother was here to see me. I would never have guessed it would be you. I thought your shame at my existence would prevent you from ever setting foot down here."

Zain greets me in the telepathic speech while he is still in the shadows. We have not so much as laid eyes on one another and already we are needling each other. I have a grim feeling about this meeting that is not at all aided by the stench of wet decay and blood that permeates the air.

"Wow!" I hear Jennifer exclaim as Zain looms out of the deep, first wrapping two big fists around the bars of his cage, then bringing the rest of his body into the pale light of the prison's meager bulbs.

He does cut an imposing figure, of that there can be no doubt. Zain's deep green hair has been cut close to his head. His tusks seem longer and more pronounced now. There are some legends that indicate our primary means of attack grow when we commit violent acts. Zain's musculature is pronounced, and the color of his skin has faded to an unhealthy underground gray. He barely seems like the same species as myself, and yet he is my full blood brother.

He looks at me and then at the human attached to me by a leash. He seems confused, as well he may be.

"What do you want?" The question is blunt and gruff and given out loud.

Jennifer takes a step toward Zain, her expression one of pure sympathy.

"How long have you been here?"

Zain looks at her. I worry he's going to curse at her or otherwise terrify her, but his expression softens. "Three years."

"I was inside for three years as well," she says. "By the time I got out, I barely believed in freedom anymore. But I found it again."

Zain takes that information in for a second.

"You're leashed to my brother."

"True," she says. "But... well. True. But that's kind of a temporary thing. I'm humoring him. He's having a hard time."

"Is he?" Zain snorts. I have not seen my brother smile in years, not since before my father passed. For a brief moment, he is his old self. He is the younger brother I have always loved and wanted to protect. I feel a pulse of connection and sadness, and I know he feels it too. It zips between us, strengthening the connection that had withered with distance and fraternal neglect.

"Oh yeah. He has.... What's his name? Kahn. He has Kahn complaining about everything. The guy cannot chill out for even a second. The first time I met me, he hit me. And that's no way to make friends, you know what I'm saying?"

"Sounds like Kahn," Zain smirks.

I feel a welling of emotion as I watch this little human who I know does not identify as mine, or my pet, do her very best to cheer Zain up simply because she knows his suffering. I should not be surprised to discover that her own species saw fit to incarcerate her at some point. My pet has a history I am yet to investigate, but she has a spirit that shines through.

"She's cute," Zain says, turning his gaze to me. "Be nice to her. Let her go."

"Yeah. Be nice. Let me go," Jennifer pipes up swiftly, knowing she has an advantage to press.

"I'm afraid that is not an option," I reply. "For either one of you."

"Then why are you here? It's not a social call, is it, Ark? You don't come to me unless you want something unspeakable done."

"I am here because I am your brother. We are family, and family must stay together."

My pet makes a gesture with a finger into her open mouth. I am briefly mystified as to the possible meaning of it, but the gagging sounds she makes soon clarify. She finds my words sickening. So does Zain, by the looks of things.

"You want something, Ark. You always want something."

"I want to see you. I want to tell you that I have not forgotten you, and will not forget you. I want you to know that I will be lobbying the council once again for a pardon. All you need do is plead guilty."

"Never."

"But you did try to kill Phenix."

"But I don't feel guilty about it."

We have had this conversation many times over the years. I knew he would not be any more remorseful this time than the others, though I had hoped he might have found some remorse in the shadows of his confinement.

"Why did you kill the guy?" My pet pipes up again, all her human curiosity very much on display.

"He killed our father. And I didn't kill him. I failed." Zain shoots another dark look at me. "Someone turned me in."

"Someone stopped you from making the biggest mistake of your life," I say. "I'm trying to stop you from perpetuating it. You don't have to spend the rest of your life in prison. You could be free with a proper expression of contrition and a suitable payment to the Wrathelders."

"Our father would turn in his premature grave if he could hear you say such things. You want to lay down and let them kill us all!"

Suddenly incensed, Zain shakes the bars with rage, his fists turning white at the knuckles with desire to burst free. Unlike my pet, Zain does not yearn for freedom. He yearns for revenge, and his presence here is not so much a punishment for him as it is the only thing preventing him from actually killing the patriarch of the Wrathelders and sparking the closest thing to civil war Euphoria has ever encountered.

J*en*

This poor fucking guy. I feel so bad for him. I wish there was some way to break him out of this horrible prison, which is a thousand times worse than the one I got stuck in. There's no real light here. There's no hope here. It feels like there's no air, either, like you could suffocate in the darkness and nobody would notice or care.

"We're going to get you out," I tell him. "That's why we're here." I glance back at Ark. "Right? To get you out."

"That's sweet, human, but you have no idea what you are talking about. Ark prefers it with me in here. It saves him the trouble of worrying about what I am doing."

"You don't belong in here."

"Jennifer..." Ark's voice comes from behind me, deep with warning.

"He doesn't. Anybody can see that. I can't even fucking see in this shitty light, and I can see that. Let's break him out!"

"Enough, pet!" Ark's tone sharpens, and his voice deepens with an authoritative bass that makes me fall silent, not with respect, but with resentment. I don't like being told to be quiet. I don't like being snapped at, either. And I especially don't like being dragged down into some fucked up alien prison to see someone who seems pretty cool suffering a fate he doesn't deserve.

Zain chuckles, but not with real amusement. It is a dark, bitter sound.

"Careful, brother," he purrs. "You can't control everybody by yelling. That one looks like a rebel, and that leash does not look strong enough to contain her when she inevitably decides that your restrictive weakness is not strength."

"Come to your senses, brother. Plead guilty. Apologize. Make amends. A time is coming when we will need all of us to be free."

I just met Zain, and I can already tell he is never going to do any of those things. I give him a little shrug. He gives me one back. We leave.

I can tell that Ark is mad. I wonder if he is more angry at his brother or at me. There is a tension I have not seen in him before. The entire time I was being returned and acting out, he was calm. Seeing his brother has riled something in him.

I wish I had the brain reading power they all seem to have. Instead, I am stuck in silence.

No sooner do we leave the cold, dark embrace of the interior of the prison than Ark starts to ring. A tone emits from somewhere near the side of his head, as an implant I wasn't aware he had comes to life.

He taps his ear and falls silent. They're talking at a distance telepathically. That's wild. I wish I had some idea what was being said. It looks important.

A*rk*

It's Kahn calling.

"Ark. I need you at the council chambers. Wrathelder has called a snap meeting. He says he's ready to launch his ships."

"Ships?"

"They've built a fleet, Ark. They've been hiding in plain sight, manufacturing dozens of human transporters. I need you up here to argue against this now, or the council is going to authorize a mass evacuation from Earth."

"Get in the vehicle." I snap the order at Jen as we reach the shuttle. My tone is sharper than it needs to be. Between Zain being the same stubborn fool as always, and Wrathelder making trouble, I am beginning to lose patience with everything and everyone.

She does as she's told. I hear her voice, small next to me. "Are you mad at me?"

"No," I say, distracted. This is all happening so quickly. It is typical of Wrathelder to strike without warning. He is an absolute monster, and if I am honest with myself, I have allowed him to gain ground. I am responsible for this, and I am going to take care of it. I am going to take care of all of it.

"We are going into a very, very important meeting," I tell my pet. "You must behave yourself. I ask that you stay by my side and remain quiet. That is all I ask."

I glance over at her, glad that I dressed her respectably today. She looks... appropriate. And that is quite a stretch from what she in fact, is, so I can consider myself fortunate that the others will not see her wildness. As long as she stays quiet, she will not be a problem, which is good, because I am about to face a great many problems.

At least we do not have to travel far to the council chambers. They are located at the very top of the same building beneath which the prison lies, so we simply rise several hundred feet and I park the shuttle again.

"This is a much nicer spot," Jen observes. It is. A large and expansive balcony extends many square miles over the city, casting a shadow that mostly falls on the prison below through an act of malicious architecture. My shuttle is surrounded by many others. Kahn was right. This is a major meeting. I haven't seen this many attendees at a meeting since my father died.

I know there is no way that Wrathelder pulled this off without creating ripples. I have allowed myself to become desensitized to the currents of the city. I have been wilfully blind and it has come at the cost of my family and perhaps my world.

As I exit the vehicle, I square my shoulders and take a deep breath. There is a light tug on the leash as my pet scrambles out behind me, straightening her skirt as she goes. In a brief glance, I can tell that she is slightly overwhelmed and still affected by our trip to the prison. I probably need to talk to her, but now is not the time. Circumstances are overhauling us.

"Come, pet," I say firmly and perhaps yes, sternly. I want her on her best behavior. She follows me obediently as we pass through the statue-filled courtyard. These effigies represent the most prominent figures of our civilization, going back hundreds of years. To have a statue here is the highest honor we have in our civilization.

On my way in, I pass the statue that bears my father, Arthas', likeness. He looks out eternally over the city, and at cross-purposes with the erstwhile patriarch of the Wrathelder clan, Diogenes.

My father was a very impressive warrior and has been depicted in his ancestral armor. A suit of the same still sits in the armory of our home. I have never had the nerve to wear it. The only one who perhaps deserves to is Zain, and he is unable to wear anything besides a prison uniform.

I aspire to his nobility and strength, but I cannot forget nor forgive the betrayal that ended his illustrious life and rendered us all bereft in the wake of it.

The sight of him strengthens me and shames me at the same time. I am not half the protector he was, and I may never be. But here, today, I will do what I need to do.

We enter the council chamber and all eyes fall upon us, briefly at least. My presence has been noted, and causes a ripple of something like consternation, especially on the other side of the chambers where Wrathelder has gathered his family.

I haven't been here in a long time. I haven't done what I should have done. I've left it all to my harassed and officious younger brother — who has just spotted me and is rushing over to greet me.

"There you are!" Kahn's expression is relieved and thunderous all at the same time. "If you missed this... even with you here. There's a real chance we're on the verge of ecocide."

"I'm here," I tell him. "And nothing is going to happen today."

I see him take a deep breath and release some of the tension he has been holding in his shoulders. I know this burden has fallen unreasonably on Kahn. That ends today.

The council chamber is a large oval space. At the head of it sits the council, nine men who represent industry, politics, technology, spirituality, environment, family, past, present, and future. Each of them has an equal vote, and for any resolution to be passed, it must be a unanimous vote. I scan their faces and relax my mind to try to catch any stray thoughts. I do not sense much of anything, but that is not surprising. They are wise and practiced in the art of schooling their minds.

I have good reason to hope that there will not be a unanimous vote today, no matter how motivated Phenix Wrathelder is.

"What's the angle?" I ask Kahn.

"He's saying it's an interplanetary emergency, that Earth needs to be evacuated in order for humanity to survive."

"When is it not a planetary emergency?"

"Exactly."

"We should take our seats. The human shouldn't be here," Kahn says, shooting an unimpressed look at Jennifer, who for once is being very quiet and very well behaved.

"I couldn't leave her alone. She won't be a problem."

Kahn looks doubtful at that, but leads me to the interlocution benches, set at the very front before the council themselves. The Wrathelders are on one side. We are on the other.

It has been almost three full years since I faced our political enemies. I thought I was calmer and more collected than Zain. I had told myself that I was above falling prey to their machinations and could not be drawn into the drama.

The moment Phenix Wrathelder makes eye contact with me, it is all I can do not to hurl myself over the table and attack him. Seeing the face of the destruction of my family is nearly too much to bear, and a large part of the reason I have avoided council matters.

Phenix is my counterpart, the eldest son of his familial dynasty. He is several years older than I am, and has the most smug, some would say noble, bearing. He has the raven hair all Wrathelders do, and the piercing blue eyes to match. I have little else to say about him and having noticed those two details is more than enough. Appearance aside, he is a venomous influence in the city, and in all likelihood the reason my father is dead. Whether he took matters into his own hands, or hired thugs to do the job for him, it makes little difference.

His two wives are flanking him. One of them is an older mate with red hair and a general air of elegance and power. The other is a beautiful, slightly younger female with hair the color of mine. One smiles blandly around at the room in general, and at the councilors especially. The other studiously avoids all eye contact, especially with Kahn and me.

I flinch as a hand touches my shoulder. Then I realize it is Kahn.

"Are you alright, brother?" There is concern in his soft tone as he chooses to use human speech instead of telepathic tongue that might be more easily intercepted by others in the room.

"I'd forgotten what it is like to face this bastard." My voice comes out in a soft growl. This is the seat of our entire civilization, and yet I feel more feral than ever. Seeing Zain mere minutes ago, having Jen by my side — a creature who may as well be a talisman of rage, being faced by my father's stone visage before entering the council chambers, it has all had an intense effect. I find myself actually struggling with self-control.

"Zain's actions seem so much more reasonable when you have to look at his face," Kahn agrees. His admission surprises me slightly. Kahn always pretends to be above these things. We both might have been putting on a show for one another.

"Is she always here?" I ask the question in low tones.

Kahn catches my eye and nods.

"Is that the man who killed your father?" Jen pipes up in the quietest voice she can muster. I had almost forgotten she was here, she has been so uncharacteristically compliant. I feel her next to me, pressed close, a warm and comforting little lump of support.

"Yes," I reply softly.

"Who are the two women?"

"His wives."

"How many fucking wives does one guy need?"

I snort gently. Phenix is greedy. One day it will be his downfall. For the moment it simply means he has far more of absolutely everything he needs, including wives.

The meeting begins when the council rises and then sits again. There are a few telepathic formalities, but they do not last long. This is an emergency meeting, apparently, and it is being treated with urgency.

Phenix Wrathelder is given the floor. Phenix stands up, immediately leaving the space behind his table, moving to claim the center of the council chambers, pacing back and forth in his black and red robes. He makes expressions of great gravity for a good long while before he actually speaks, as if trying to impress us with the great depth of his thoughts.

"Hurry up, dickhead," Jen mumbles under her breath. I feel her next to me, squirming impatiently. Putting a hand on her leg seems to calm her, but I can feel the tension in her body almost as well as I feel the tension in mine.

Phenix's first words are an outrageous exaggeration. He chooses to speak in human tongue as well. Perhaps he is trying to demonstrate his own proficiency in that language.

"We have called this emergency meeting because Earth is in an emergency. Humanity is in an emergency."

"Are we?" Jen mutters next to me. I nudge her to encourage quiet.

"They suffer in filth, they are subject to violence. They are unable to govern themselves effectively and there has not been a day since they were conceived of that they have ever known peace. The humans of Earth live short, brutal lives of savagery."

He turns around to gesture at my brother and me, and Jen.

"The house of Voros claims to love humanity, but they only ever save a few of them at best, picking a small number of humans to be pets, ensuring their profit margins remain obscenely high and controlling the market! Wrathelders wish to truly save humanity, and that means bringing as many here as possible, not to mention, making humans affordable for every Euphorian who wishes to own one, or perhaps two, or an entire breeding family!"

There is a cheer from those in the public gallery who are no doubt shareholders in Wrathelder's companies and more specifically, in this new venture. This meeting is tactically stacked to try to sway the council. I can admit, if I knew nothing about Earth, I might very well be swayed by the passion of Phenix's argument. It sounds reasonable if you know nothing about anything.

Suddenly, in the midst of his stirring conclusion, a voice comes from very near my elbow. It is loud and strident.

"Oh fuck off!"

Jen is on her feet. Jen is on her feet, on the table. She moved with a speed impressive for anybody, let alone a human. I reach to grab her, but she jumps forward over the table, forgetting the leash. It snaps hard around her neck, and mercifully breaks.

My pet is now loose in the council chambers. She rushes up to Phenix, and though she is just barely over half his height, somehow still manages to get in his face.

"We're not savages, and we're not suffering. He's talking complete bullshit. I've been trying to get back to Earth since I came here. Why would I do that if it was an emergency there?"

Phenix turns to the council, and then to the audience with a smug smirk on his face.

"Typical. Arkan Voros brings his trained pet here to parrot lies to you all. Her words prove my point. Not his."

An expression of outrage and horror crosses Jen's pretty face. "Do I look trained to you, bitch?"

There is a collective gasp at her blunt and bold rudeness.

"Arkan Voros, control your human!" The chairman of the council, Kento Fosgrip, makes the demand. His green and gold hair flows about his head in offended waves as he shakes that same head in disapproval.

"I'M NOT HIS HUMAN. I'm MY human!" Jennifer practically explodes.

Phenix's expression is smug and patronizing as he chooses to wind her up further, turning a scene into a spectacle. "You're a trained little monkey, dancing to…"

He gets what he wants. We never get to hear the end of Phenix's insult, because Jen jumps to give herself momentum and reach, and drives her small fist right into his nose, busting it open in a cascade of very unbecoming blood.

Phenix Wrathelder, patriarch of his name, staggers backwards, shocked. He's never been hit in the face before. Not like this. Not in front of every respectable member of society. Not by a diminutive human woman who refuses to take his arrogance and has less than no respect for him.

"That's for Zain," she says, immediately making the entire situation exponentially worse by referencing our most murderous and criminal sibling.

I cannot let this continue. I vault the table and whip her up into my arms, tossing her over my shoulder where she continues to taunt Phenix, who has retreated to his wives with his nose bleeding all down the front of him. It is now Jen's turn to taunt him.

"What's wrong? Want to declare a state of emergency, you fucking pussy? You come to Earth, you're going to get more of that."

I slap her ass, but not as hard as I should, and I hand her over to Kahn.

"Take her out of here," I tell him. "I'll fix this."

Kahn gives me a furious look, but he does as I ask. Jen shouts the whole time she is being carried out of the chamber, even as loud shot-like sounds emanate from where Kahn's palm sharply meets her upturned ass.

Once they are gone and order is restored, all eyes are on me, expecting me to explain myself and apologize for Jennifer. I do neither. Instead, I take my opportunity.

"This is what you are asking for. Tens, perhaps hundreds of thousands of these. Not the well-trained, cosseted pets you love, but the kind of human you just saw. Untrained, wild humans who decide their own fate, who not only do not respect our authority, but will wage full-scale war against it. Who breed at a nearly uncontrollable and absolutely exponential rate. Who may very well represent an invasion force. One small female assaulted a high-ranking member of a prominent family in full view of the council and was able to pass his guard. Can you imagine what a veritable horde of them could do? We make humans our pets through careful selection and training. What we do cannot be replicated en masse, and anybody who is arrogant enough to think so will soon end up with more than a bloody nose."

There is silence after I speak, but I can see the reactions of the council, and the muted reception from the stacked balconies is telling. The cute, sweet little humans they are accustomed to seeing as pets are not representative of the population as a whole, as Jen inadvertently demonstrated today.

Wrathelder is beaten, and he knows it. The expression on his face is violent. I can only imagine how much his fleet is going to cost him while it is sitting in dry-dock. This has been a day of great triumph for the house of Voros. We have bloodied Wrathelder's nose literally and metaphorically. The story of what happened here is already spreading among the population. I feel mirth in the outer edges of my mind. He planned to undercut us today, and he has become a laughingstock in the process.

I walk to Phenix and lean into him, outwardly making a physical show of apology and comfort. As I close the distance so only he and I can hear, I choose to speak in human words, not thoughts.

"Clean yourself up. You're a mess."

Then I look behind him, and finally make eye contact with his wife, the one who shares my hair, my eyes, my very DNA.

"Mother." I bow my head briefly before taking my leave.

7

Jen

I am dragged out of the meeting with my ass being beaten, and I don't fucking care. I'd do everything I just did all over a hundred more times if it meant punching that asshole in the face again. My knuckles are throbbing, but it was worth it. Nobody talks about my home and my species that way and gets away with it.

"Why did you do that?" Kahn is astonished. I can tell he has no idea what to do with me, now we are out by the vehicle. He puts me down and holds me by the short remainder of leash that is still attached to my collar.

"You're going to need a chain," he mutters to himself before I can answer.

"I did it for Zain," I say as I feel the displaced tug.

Kahn stares at me askance. "How do you know Zain?"

"I met him right before we came here. Ark took me."

Kahn's expression refuses to resolve into comprehension. "You attacked someone for a man you met an hour ago?"

"I'd punch that guy for someone I never met. He has a very punchable face. And even more punchable words."

Kahn's lips quirk for a moment as if he is tempted to show amusement, but the expression is gone as swiftly as it came. "You cannot commit violence."

"Why not? You did. First thing you did when you met me."

"That's different. You deserved..."

He stops talking, because we both know the guy I just punched in the face deserved it too.

"You're trouble," he says. "And we have enough of that to go around already."

"Perfect. Put me on a shuttle back to Earth. That's all I've been asking for since I got to your shitty planet."

"Language!" Kahn snaps the word.

"What about it?"

I see his hands flex, and I know he wants nothing more than to grab me and start whipping my ass. But he doesn't. He keeps hold of my leash and he looks in the direction of the council chambers. He's waiting for Ark.

Ark must have told him he's not allowed to touch me.

That creates an opportunity for some real mayhem. A smile spreads across my face and just keeps getting wider.

"Don't look so pleased with yourself. When Arkan is able to get you alone, you will pay the price."

"Maybe, but unless and until he does, I'm untouchable. Aren't I." My smile only grows wider as I speak those words aloud and see them confirmed in Kahn's gold-flecked gaze. My cheeks are starting to hurt from sheer smugness.

"You're not untouchable. Keep this up, and you'll find out."

"Or you will, if you touch me and Ark finds out."

A hard slap bursts across my ass. I yowl and jump in surprise, turning to see Ark standing behind me, tall and imposing and clearly unimpressed by my behavior.

"Let's get out of here before it occurs to anyone to impound this human brat," he growls, talking over my head to Kahn.

I am bundled into the shuttle between Kahn and Ark. We swiftly make an exit from the city, skimming at what seems to me to be a much faster than usual speed. Conversation is sparse and tense, but I don't think their anger, or whatever emotions are driving them are directed at me. I think they're worried about the asshole whose blood is drying under my fingernails.

"Don't worry about that guy," I say, breaking the silence. "He's a little bitch."

"Thank you for your input on the situation," Kahn says dryly.

"He is a little bitch, though," Ark agrees, just as dryly.

The tension is broken as both alien men laugh at that description of someone who I gather has become quite a loathed and maybe even feared enemy to them. I wish I understood more. I wish we'd broken the third brother out of prison. Thinking about him in that darkness makes me sick. I know what it's like to be captured in that way. What's happening to me now is nothing compared to the desperation of being behind bars.

We are soon home. Ark takes me by the hand, rather than by the broken leash, and takes me up to his bedroom. I know I am in trouble. I feel the quivering of something like guilt, but more like excitement in my belly as he lets me go and closes the door behind me.

I can already tell that he's not actually angry at me. Neither of the brothers are. Not that I care what Kahn thinks. I wouldn't mind if Kahn was angry. It would be funny as hell. I don't know if I would enjoy Ark's displeasure as much.

"That was quite a day," Ark says. "It would have challenged even a well-trained pet. You are not well-trained, but you will receive more training now."

He's being very composed, very professional. I can tell he wants me to take this seriously. But I am distracted by him, his physical presence, his masterful demeanor. And his tall, broad, hot fucking alien body.

I bite my lower lip and look up at him under my lashes. "Did anybody ever tell you that you're really handsome when you're stern?"

His deep blue brows lower just a fraction over slightly narrowed golden eyes. "You won't seduce your way out of this, pet."

"I'm sorry," I say, not sorry at all. I lower my eyes in a facsimile of submission, which directs my gaze toward his crotch, where I see the evidence that my appreciation has created a response of the turgid alien cock kind.

"You can stop smiling like that," he lectures. "And you can remove those clothes. They were pristine when you put them on. Now look at them."

"Covered in the blood of your enemies, as they should be," I say without shame.

He smiles, and I see pride and affection in his visage, and I know, without a shadow of a doubt, I am not in proper trouble.

"You are something, Jennifer," he says. "Tell me, why were you imprisoned?"

An invisible shadow is cast over the proceedings. I was so very in the moment with him until he brought that up. There are some things in a person's life that are best forgotten if at all possible. Part of the reason I punched the alien in the face was to discharge the anxiety that built up when we were down in the alien jail. It worked too.

Now it's back.

Silence draws out between us. I wait for him to get the hint and move on with the conversation. I'd rather he was whipping my ass than asking these questions. But he doesn't move the conversation on, and I can't exactly make him spank me.

"You can tell me, Jennifer," he says in a rare instance of using my name. It makes me feel warm and maybe a little safe. I guess I can trust him. I suppose I don't really have a choice.

"They said I killed someone."

"And did you?"

"I don't know. Maybe a little."

He folds his arms over his broad chest, scales gleaming. "How do you kill someone a little?"

I shrug.

"Alright. Well, now I understand why you wanted to help Zain out of prison."

"Sounds to me like he tried to kill someone who needed killing."

"Phenix perhaps deserves death, but it was never Zain's job to mete out that justice. I do not know the circumstances of your crime..."

"Fuck off."

"Excuse me?"

"It's not a crime to kill someone who deserves it. Laws are threats made by people with power. They're not anything actually real. I don't recognize laws. And I don't care about crime. I know what's right and wrong for me. I bet Zain does too."

Ark's eyes narrow just a little more. "That's an interesting perspective, but there are some laws you will follow now. Mine. I will enforce them. And you will not attack anybody from now on. It could be dangerous for you, and for us.

Now. Take off those bloody clothes and go and get in the bath."

I find myself losing my temper. This isn't fair. He could at least congratulate me a little.

"I'll punch him again if I get a chance," I say on my way past. "You know, some people would be grateful to find out that someone they recently captured and beat still had their back for no reason. You're a fucking tyrant, no different from the other guy, really."

A*rk*

It takes a lot of self-control not to grab her and just thrash her, especially given her complete lack of contrition. This pet knows how to push buttons. More than that, she knows how to break faces.

I don't really want to punish her. Not for punching Phenix, anyway. She's giving me plenty of other reasons, like that sassy attitude that persists in the face of imminent punishment.

Spanking her is not making an impression. She's a tougher candidate than that. Her mouth and her actions are creating situations that her tender rear cannot possibly atone for. There is only so much beating any human can take, even one who deserves a lifetime of them.

It occurs to me that I do have some technology that might help in this situation. It is experimental, and I know she'll loathe it, but I need her under control. So far I clearly have no control at all.

I open a drawer in my room that I did not imagine I would be opening anytime soon. There is a device inside, a rather unassuming little piece of equipment. When this was designed, it was quickly considered to be far too intense a punishment for all but the most resistant pets. Kahn and I had a better eye for potential pets, and so it remained something we never used on any of those we trained for the market.

There is the sound of water and splashing and a fair amount of grumbling and cursing as I wait. I will give my pet some credit, she has actually followed my instructions and is washing herself.

A few minutes later, she struts out of the bathroom, naked and glistening with remnants of bathwater. She is beautiful, a curvaceous creature without remorse or obvious conscience. A pretty little monster. *My* pretty little monster.

She sees the device immediately, just as I intended.

"What is that? Looks like a dildo."

"It is a toy of sorts, pet. Would you like to play with it?"

I am using her cockiness against her, and I can see instantly in her eyes that she is going to take the bait.

J*en*
What Ark's got looks like a dildo with a few extra pieces. Seems there's a bit that tickles the clit, and another extrusion ready to slide into the butt. It looks like a filthy fucking toy, and hell yeah I want to play with it.

"Lie down on the bed on your back," Ark orders.

He puts the toy down into some kind of case by the bed and takes the opportunity to remove his shirt. I love the way his belly looks, rippling with muscles bordered by scales. He is dangerous and handsome as hell, and I cannot resist him. I did not get to see him properly naked yet. This is the first time I am beholding him in all his true alien glory — and it is glorious. There is an unscaled swathe of chest and belly, and they are powerfully built. These aliens are built for battle, but they act like they're knitting circle members. I know Arkan has a primal side. I want to see it. I want to feel it. I want him to fuck me with it.

"And the pants too?" I make the suggestion with an arch little giggle.

He raises a brow, and for a second I think he is going to refuse, but he obliges me, stripping as naked as I am. As I see his thighs and thick alien cock come into view, I forget about everything remotely resembling trouble. He is the sexiest thing I have ever seen. He has thick legs, scaled on the outside and up around his pubic region. The base of his cock has light scales, and the rest of it is a rapidly engorging rod that I remember from feel if not from sight.

When I take in all of him from the top of his flowing blue hair, to his golden gaze, to the slight shine of feral tusks and then a body made for aggression and defense in equal measure, I forget about absolutely everything other than my raw desire for him.

"Lay down." He reminds me of his earlier order, and I do not hesitate to obey.

I crawl up onto the large bed on hands and knees and lie down on my back looking up at him, preparing myself for pleasure. He and I both know that I really deserve a reward for what I did today. I helped him talk to his brother — it was pretty awkward between them before I spoke up. And I definitely helped him when I punched his enemy.

I am feeling very much in control now. He will serve me sexually. He will give me pleasure, and we will give up this pretense of pet and master now that he knows what I am capable of.

Blue hair falls forward over his muscular shoulders and I fucking melt as he crawls onto the end of the bed. The head of his cock is spearing toward me even at a distance. I crave him inside me, and I can see from the lust in his eyes that he wants me just as much. There is an intensity in his gaze as he crawls toward me, this big, fanged alien predator who lives his life in a veneer of political respectability. I see the animal in him, and I see how he wants to break the wild thing in me. He wants me kept. He wants me contained. He wants me leashed. He wants me caged.

He's welcome to try.

He has the alien sex toy in hand as he reaches the place between my thighs where my natural lubrication is making me ready for him. He activates the thing with the pad of his thumb. It lights up and begins to vibrate in a way that seems very promising. Again I am reassured that I'm not going to be punished. I'm going to be pleasured.

"Spread your legs," he orders in his rough alien tongue.

I am only too happy to obey, parting my thighs to give him easy access to the wet core of me. My ass still bears the memory of all yesterday's punishments, but that pain only seems to encourage my arousal. I never considered myself a masochist, but maybe I am. As the buzzing, thrumming tip of the toy makes its way slowly down the seam of my lips, it finds the little pool of wetness where I am ready to be taken.

I let out a moan of anticipation as the vibrations begin to resonate through me. He pushes the toy forward slowly, but firmly, stretching me open.

The tip of the toy is reaching for my clit. I feel it lightly tickling, and though it is yet to make proper contact with my pussy, it is making the air move, and that air is caressing and teasing the taut little bud hiding at the apex of my lower lips.

Ark pushes his tool another inch or so inside me and suddenly I am jolted with a powerful burst of erotic energy that seems to emanate from the toy and find every single nerve and nerve ending in my body. It is a kind of pleasure no simple physical stimulus could provide. There's something electric happening, or some other kind of energy. I don't know what, but it's powerful. It's like an instant orgasm delivered in the blink of an eye and gone as quickly.

"What was that!?" I gasp.

"Your punishment," Ark says, taking advantage of my softened state to press the toy all the way home, filling my pussy and breaching my ass in one firm thrust. I feel my ass stretch around the thick alien plastic. There is a thicker bulb at the end of the probe and then it narrows so my ass is not stretched super wide at the muscular ring, but will be stretched and stretched again when the toy is thrust in and out of me. The whimper I emit at this realization turns into a moan as the softer tendrils designed to suck against my clit and inner lips begins. Every part of my sex is under alien control, every erogenous part of me under direct threat of stimulation.

"My punishment?" I just barely breathe the question as I feel every part of me start to vibrate again.

"Yes," Ark says. He is over me, covering me with his body, resting his weight on one arm while the other manipulates the toy inside me, thrusting it in and out with a slow but steady pace.

It feels as though it is swelling inside me, growing larger and larger with every passing thrust. I would have said such a thing was impossible, but this is alien technology and I suppose I have no real idea how it works. I can feel it though, turning me into a writhing, squirming, moaning sexual mess.

"You will obey me, pet," Ark intones, his voice thick with lust and determination.

Before I can reply in the negative, another orgasm bursts through me, but this time it is not a brief pulse. This time it is a soul-shattering crescendo of pure pleasure that makes my vision blur and a raw scream escape my mouth. It lasts much longer than any orgasm I have ever had in my life. It rolls on for what feels like a small eternity before he allows it to fade again.

"You will do as you are told, you will bend your will to mine, you will follow my instructions, and most importantly, you will be a good girl." He emphasizes every single one of his words with a thrust of that infernal toy, fucking me with it through the aftermath of the most complete orgasmic experience of my existence.

"Do you understand, pet?"

I make an incoherent sound. Not the right kind of sound though, because he flicks that switch on the toy. Electric sensations ensue, stimulating my tight ass, making the inner walls of my pussy contract and release in swift succession, and my clit is strummed by agile alien fingers that heighten the entire experience. It is my third orgasm in as many minutes, and I cannot stop screaming.

When he finally lets me settle again, I feel an intense ache between my thighs and in my ass and even in my clit. I am left whimpering for mercy. I try to reach down and pull the toy out of my holes, but he predictably and quite casually slaps my hand away.

"Oh no," he says. "This is not over until I decide it is over. You are going to be disciplined thoroughly tonight. You are going to learn what it is to obey so there is not another shameful scene in the council chambers or anywhere else. Promise obedience, pet, or you will continue to suffer pleasure."

I part my lips, knowing I should tell him what he wants to hear. I should promise to be good. I should swear to submit to him. But I can't. Not even now, covered in sweat, with my thighs and hands both trembling with the effort of repeated orgasms.

Ark lets out a low growl, makes direct fucking eye contact with me, and flicks the switch One. More. Time.

I scream as I come again, writhing so much Ark is forced to move his body so he has an arm free to pin me down by the throat, keeping me in place with a leg thrown over one of mine. My thighs are parted, my hips are arched, my nipples are rock hard and absolutely aching along with every pulse of my clit.

"FUCK!" I shriek the word.

"Submit, pet," Ark growls, showing his true dominant nature. I have misjudged him. He is smart and he is cultured, and he has a way about him that makes him seem wholesome and maybe even harmless.

He is not harmless. Not even a little.

He is a monster, and I am fortunate to be his pet. Were I not his pet, I would surely be his prey. As I stare up into his fanged face through a rictus of forced orgasm, I am stunned at how blind I have been.

I can't resist him. He won't ever let me go. He will make me come until I submit to him. I know that as surely as I have ever known anything.

"I SUBMIT!"

Tears start to leak from my eyes even as those words leave my mouth. I am humiliated, but I cannot blame anybody but myself. He gave me every chance to follow his orders, and I didn't.

Finally, Ark pulls the toy from my pussy. It seems as though he is showing me mercy, but he almost immediately replaces it with his cock, surging inside my pussy with a rough, dominating thrust that fills me all the way to my very depths.

Ark fucks me hard, pinning me to the bed and pounding his hips against mine, using me, claiming me, giving me a proper animal fucking. I am unable to reciprocate his vigor because every bit of energy I had has already been drained by his alien toy. I lie beneath my alien master, and I am fucked like an object. My pussy grips his cock even though I am exhausted, my inner walls aching and yet still wrapped tight around his alien rod.

"Mine," he snarls down at me, pressing a rough alien fanged kiss to my mouth.

"Mine," he repeats, thrusting his hips against mine and grinding his cock deep inside me, pushing the head of his cock so far inside me it feels as though I am nothing more than a puppet for his rod.

"Mine," he says one more time, pulling free entirely, gripping my hips between his big, scaled hands, sliding up to his knees and dragging me after him. My ass is pulled over his scaled thighs, and I feel their texture igniting the old spanking marks as he sheaths his cock inside me and proceeds to use me like a fuck doll, pulling my tight cunt on and off his cock with ever faster thrusts.

I wail and writhe as I do what I said I would do: submit to my alien master and his rough lovemaking. I know now that there is nothing Ark would not do to get me under control.

He comes inside me with a roar of triumphant domination, his seed filling me up to the absolute brim. I feel it dripping out of me even before he pulls completely free of my aching, well-fucked pussy and allows me to slide back down onto the bed before him, my legs still open, his cum now dripping from my aching pussy all over his sheets.

For a long moment, there is nothing but the sound of his heavy breathing and my own light whimpering.

"You're beautiful," Ark says. "I already want to fuck you again."

That confession of his makes me whine softly.

Ark puts his hands on my hips and turns me over onto my stomach. I feel myself being pulled back again, thighs parted around his thighs. The head of his cock finds what used to be the tight bud of my ass. He uses the seed and semen of his cum to lubricate me for another fucking. This time it is my ass that receives his cock, my rear spreading for him the same way my cunt did.

I whimper and whine all the way through my ass fuck. Ark performs his mating slowly and deliberately, no longer motivated by rash lust. He has himself under control now. He has me under control as well. I feel him inside not just my ass, but inside my head. I'm never going to be able to give him attitude the same way again, not without remembering how it felt to have him fuck my ass with these deliberate, disciplinary strokes, occasionally spanking my rear relatively lightly. He doesn't need to be overly forceful now. He's made his point. Now he's simply using my ass as a sort of after-punishment cool down.

"Such a good girl," he praises me as he keeps me clamped on his cock. "Such a good little pet. I am enjoying your pussy and your ass very much, pet. I will use them both often, and you will present them for my use when I ask. Understand?"

I nod in the affirmative as hot tears run down my cheeks. They are not tears of pain or debasement, but rather tears of actual remorse. His punishment has changed something in me.

Ark

rk

Is it wrong to fuck her ass as she cries? In any general sense, probably, but my pet needs to know I am capable of truly disciplining her. Little spankings and plain warnings have not sufficed at all. But this? This is working admirably. She is soft and she is supple, and much of the fight that she has been carrying since I met her has finally retreated, leaving the rest of her in a much calmer state.

Am I enjoying inflicting this deserved cruelty? Yes, if I am to be honest with myself I am. Usually I am very careful to be tender yet firm with humans. I certainly do not ravage them into submission. But this one is different. This one is reckless and impulsive and demands a proper breaking.

Her soft sniffles are quite adorable, making my cock stay entirely stiff even in the direct aftermath of orgasm as I fuck her all the way through a second climax of my own. It might seem excessive, but she came multiple times and it seems only fair I should orgasm at least twice.

I come again, inside her ass this time. My pleasure is in direct proportion to her punished submission, especially as I release her and let her slide off my cock, leaking my seed from both her naughty human holes.

"Oh my..." She lies before me, curled up slightly on the rucked-up sheets. Her face and much of her body is flushed with a deeper pink hue that would usually indicate some kind of slap or light trauma, but this is the human color of shame — and I hope, also submission.

"You were a naughty pet today," I say. "And yesterday, and most of the days before. But you are forgiven now."

Jen

Is this what forgiveness feels like? A hot and aching ass and a body so wrung out from alien orgasm that I can barely think? I'm hardly listening to his words. They are a soft rumble of sound, accompanied by a surprisingly tender massaging of large alien hands over all the parts most recently punished.

I should hate him for what he just did, but I don't. I can't. Because how I feel now is astonishingly good. It is as though I have been forced through some internal wall and found an ocean of calm on the other side of it.

I lie in bed as my alien master fetches warm cloths and whatever alien salves might be used to heal a punished pet and applies both to the nether regions of my body.

I will sleep well tonight. I will sleep well right fucking now.

8

"Phenix Wrathelder is here to see you, Ark."

My brother's voice is tense and extremely formal as it comes floating up the stairs, preceding him only slightly.

It is the afternoon of the day following our triumph before the council, and we had been relaxing. There had been an air of warmth and comfort about the house, a general sense of contentment that has been absent for quite some time.

It dissipates the moment Kahn says Wrathelder's name.

I marvel at the nerve of Phenix to dare come to our property and set foot on the soil of my father's name.

I had been relaxing with my pet on the balcony overlooking the gardens. She has been very soft and very compliant today. I have praised her many times for the shift in her attitude. It would be saying too much to say she had changed completely, but there is no doubt the beginnings of transformation from wild to tame are in place. A precedent has been set. She is aware now of some of the lengths I will go to in order to ensure her obedience, and simply knowing them seems to have calmed her a great deal.

Phenix's appearance at our door besmirches what I had hoped would be a much needed day of rest for the house of Voros.

"In your crate, pet," I order my human. I do not want her loose while he is here. The temptation to punch him in the face would no doubt be too extreme. I am already feeling intensely annoyed by his presence, which I know is a harbinger of trouble. For Phenix Wrathelder to set foot in the heart of our territory is an act of boldness I can barely comprehend, especially given how thoroughly beaten he was yesterday.

Jen slinks into her crate with only a slight look of resentment in her pretty eyes. I know she wants to see her handiwork, but I must deny her that pleasure. What training I have managed to instill in her could easily be undone by one moment of triumph.

I dress myself and go downstairs to meet our uninvited guest. I feel the satisfaction I decided it was best to deny my pet as I reach the bottom of the stairs and find him with Kahn.

Phenix has been mended as best as is possible, but there is a swelling about his nose and a certain darkness around his left eye. My little human did significant damage to a member of an allegedly superior species.

"To what do we owe this honor?" I keep my demeanor welcoming.

"I wanted to thank you, Arkan," Phenix says.

"Oh?"

Phenix's eyes are gleaming with malevolence. "Your display yesterday finally convinced my investors, and several key members of the council to invest in a new program."

"Oh?"

I refuse to be drawn into any further conversational gambits. He has come here smug and with a self-satisfied air I do not trust.

"You see, humans have been regarded as amusements, fashionable accessories, a fad, a trend..."

I listen, knowing that he would not be here if it were not to see my face when he twists the knife I do not yet know he has inside me.

Within the next few sentences, that suspicion is entirely confirmed.

"Your human, sweet, and small, and very female as she is, demonstrated an aspect of humanity that has gone unregarded by council. Their capacity for ruthless, senseless, and explosive violence."

I do not reply at all this time when he pauses. I let him have his dramatic little moment.

"I want you to hear this from me, Voros," he says, his lips curling with dark and vengeful delight. You will have it confirmed by the council soon enough I am sure, but I asked if I might be the one to bring you the news in person, out of respect for your investment and contributions to human research."

Another pause. Another silence.

"The human pet trade is being put on indefinite hold. After all, these creatures are erratic in nature and could very well pose a danger to families, especially those with children."

He lets that sink in for a moment, before twisting a second metaphorical blade. These barbs are exceptionally sharp. I suppose I should be grateful they are merely words and not actual blades like the ones driven into my father's flesh at his behest.

"Wrathelders have been awarded the contract to import humans. Not as pets, but as guard animals."

Rage swims in my heart and in my eyes and threatens to taint my tongue. I make a great effort of self-control to keep my response short and bland.

"You have no experience with humans."

"We have plenty of experience in matters of war. The council saw your failure in taming that human you brought into their presence. Blood was spilled for all to see. Really, it was a very poor decision on your part. They saw how you had indulged her and allowed her to become untamed and dangerous. They were on the verge of demanding all humans be retrieved and destroyed for public safety. We intervened on their behalf."

"And I was not consulted on this because…"

"Because you were the one who brought the entire matter to a head. Your family has a reputation for recklessness and violence, Voros. You know that. Look at your father…"

Finally, I speak properly, saying the words that live inside me, words that have waited far too long to be given voice.

"Phenix. If I see you again, I will kill you. Get out of my house."

The smug smile disappears from his visage, because there is an abundance of meaning and intent in my words. They are not idle threats. I am on the verge of killing him myself, in this very moment, while he stands in my home taking advantage of my hospitality.

If I were to kill him, I would take Zain's place in prison. My life would be over, as his would be. It would serve nothing, solve nothing, but suddenly the ancient part of my being is activated. The old warrior roars. My ancestors demand blood, and restitution.

He sees death in my eyes and takes a few sensible steps backward.

I am not done speaking.

"If war is what you want with me, Phenix, war is what you will have. I have forgiven you at every turn. I have allowed you to continue to exist where my brothers would have preferred you in the ground. And now you come to me, in my home, and you effectively beg for death. Is that what you want? Are you tired of life?"

"You are emotional," Phenix says. "This is why I came to tell you in person. The council would not look kindly on one of your Voros tantrums. Your father..."

I snarl and dart forward. Kahn steps between us, saving Phenix from a set of tusk wounds.

"Please leave," Kahn reiterates.

Kahn is the calmest of all of us, the most sensible. I am glad he has come to cool the situation down. Then I realize he is holding an axe. Where did he get that from?

Phenix looks at the pair of us and decides to push his luck that little bit further.

"You boys are not the men your father was..."

"It's like you actually want me to hit you with this axe," Kahn observes. "And it's almost as though you don't think I haven't thought of a thousand different ways to kill you, and a thousand more ways to make it look like an accident."

"Bold, bald threats from two boys who should know better than to imagine I have come here unobserved. Keep your temper, children."

With that, Phenix takes his leave. He has undoubtedly bested us on every level, and letting him walk out of my home alive feels like a humiliation almost too deep to bear.

I am sure his family knows where he is. Our conversation has probably been recorded through some device in his clothing, because he is the sort of creature who would do that. I am certain, now I think about it, that our home is likely surrounded by armed guards, a small militia ready to take everything from us in one bloodbath.

Yet again, we have been played like instruments, dull ones, like drums. Phenix now probably has fresh evidence of contemporary death threats from our house. If anything happens to him, suspicion will fall directly upon us, and ruin will surely follow.

"What is wrong with us?" Kahn asks the question when we are certain Phenix has finally departed. "We go to absolute pieces around that man."

"There's nothing wrong with us. Nothing besides the fact we have allowed evil to walk this world for too long, and we have made the mistake of confronting it directly when it always moves in shadow. We have tried peace. It is time we did what we should have done three years ago."

"And what is that?"

"First, we are going to break Zain out of prison."

"We're... what?" Kahn looks completely taken aback.

"We're going to break Zain out of prison. I see no reason why our brother should continue to languish in the so-called justice of this clearly corrupt state. If Phenix has the council in his pocket, then all semblance of fairness is gone. Their decision was in our favor yesterday, and today he claims to have all he wished for, in addition to having destroyed our own efforts. We are at war, Kahn. We have tried to avoid the fact, but we cannot any longer. Phenix is going to destroy us if we let him, and I refuse to let that happen."

"Hell, yeah!"

I turn around to see Jennifer standing on the stairs behind me. She has put some clothes on from the collection of pet outfits I keep. She's chosen a black bustier and matching leather pants and boots. It was an outfit conceived of by Zain before he went to prison, and never put into production as most of our species prefers their pets to look a little softer. Combined with her naturally rebellious demeanor, it is a striking ensemble.

"How did you..."

"Your crates *really* suck," she reminds me.

So much for having broken her to my will yesterday. It seems as though her forced orgasmic submission was only short term in nature. I find myself quite unconcerned by this revelation. I am glad, in fact.

Kahn does not share my pleasure.

"She should be contained," Kahn says. "And so should Zain. The last thing we need now are reckless rebels causing chaos."

"I disagree. I think that is exactly what we need. The council has turned. They may have turned a long time ago. Who knows how deep the corruption runs? Our father's death was not honorable. He was set on in a place he should have been safe, outnumbered, and left to die from wounds inflicted by cowards who have never been caught. How is that possible in a civilization of justice?"

Jen

Ark is fuming. I have never seen him so agitated. I've only been in his presence for a couple of days, but they have been an intense couple of days. I'm starting to think this rich, privileged family of aliens needs someone like me around. They're so busy trying to play by the rules of their world they don't even notice when they're getting fucked. He notices now that his enemies are at his door, and that being good has gotten him nowhere.

I feel like I have a purpose here, like the universe wants me to be part of overthrowing this fucked up society that pretends to be advanced but is obviously rotten to the core.

"Fuck civilization," I say.

Kahn groans. "We need to get ourselves together, calm down, and not react to this obvious attempt to make us lose our cool. It is not ideal that Wrathelder is able to import humans en masse, nor is it good that our own licenses have been suspended — if that is truly the case. But becoming lawless, murderous rogues will not help matters."

"I vote for becoming lawless and murderous," I pipe up.

"You don't get a vote, pet. You will get the belt if you don't go back to your crate this instant," Kahn says.

"You're not my master, Kahn. Ark is, and he wants me here."

Ark takes a deep, stabilizing breath, and sighs. "Kahn's right. We cannot afford to lose our cool. We must make tactical steps…"

"I am glad you are seeing sense," Kahn says.

"… to free Zain from prison, and restore our family name."

"No," Kahn groans as I laugh. "She's a pet. She's a human. She's not someone to take advice from. You know better than this, Ark."

"Do I. Do you? Are we sensible? Or are we being pathetic and weak? Our father is dead, and our mother warms our enemy's bed."

"That son of a bitch is fucking your mom?" I exclaim, shocked. I knew something was going on in that council room. There was a weird tension that didn't seem right, even for adversarial aliens. So Phenix is literally a smug motherfucker. Makes sense.

"Our mother felt the Wrathelders were better able to provide for her needs in the wake of my father's passing," Kahn says. "It was a choice she was free to make."

Kahn's tone is one of barely contained rage when he speaks about his mother's treachery, and I instantly know that's the key to getting him on my side. I've now forgotten completely about getting back to Earth. Avenging Ark's family's honor seems like a much more satisfying time. I'm the sort of girl who does best when she has a mortal enemy.

"So, free Zain, then kill Phenix Wrathelder, stop the mass-transit of humans from Earth. How hard can it be?" I tick the items off, one on each of my fingers.

Kahn growls at me. "We are supposed to be training her, not drawing her into a potential civil war. There are reasons we stayed our hand, Ark. It was father's final wish for there to be peace on Euphoria."

Ark replies in a deep, feral growl. "Was it? Do we know what his final wish was as he bled out on the blades of traitors?"

Ark is so fucking hot right now, his orc-like tusks chomping at the air, as his dragonesque, near fae appearance only serves as a foil for the brutality emerging from within. The contrast of his incredible strength and potential wildness with the trappings of his collected civilization is turning me the hell on. He is not done making his plans, either.

"Do not worry, brother. *I* will train her. Jen, if you are going to be a part of this plan, you will have to become obedient. I have to know when I send you into battle, you will do as you are told."

"Into battle," I repeat. I like the sound of that.

"She's a soft, small human. She has no place in battle," Kahn objects.

"Metaphorically, Kahn. If we do this correctly, there will be no wars waged. We will act swiftly. Jen will be a distraction. Nothing more. No harm will come to her. We can take Wrathelder down while they imagine they have won."

"What could possibly go wrong," Kahn deadpans.

With those words, he gives in.

9

Ark

Three days have passed since Phenix came to our home and a plan has been arrived at. It is not one that pleases Kahn, but he has agreed to go along with it. We must move swiftly if we are to stop Wrathelder. Word is that he is launching his ship to Earth this very day. It is going to be a spectacle with much fanfare, being a vast and impressive piece of engineering.

News of his achievements has dominated media. The papers are full of him. As we walk through the streets of Eutopia, I see person after person with their heads buried in the same glossy communications screens with the same lead story scrolling across them.

TITAN WILL FERRY HUMANITY TO A NEW AND BRIGHTER FUTURE!

The headline is followed by a picture of Phenix standing next to the massive ship with a very broad grin on his face.

They've altered the image so you cannot see the black eye Jennifer gave him.

I am grateful to be surrounded by reminders of why we are going to do what we are about to do. In the modern history of Eutopia, nobody of any breeding has ever acted contrary to the will and law of the council. That is about to change today.

The prison that holds our brother is widely regarded to be impenetrable, but nothing in this world or any other is truly impenetrable. It is time we got Zain free.

"What's the plan, again?" Jen asks the question slightly nervously, as well she might. She will play a role in this, and she will make a sacrifice.

"You know the plan," I reassure her.

"Sure," she giggles a little. "The plan is going to hurt."

I have her on a light chain now that it is clear she is more than capable of breaking lighter restraints.

I look down at her as we stroll around the perimeter of the inner spire, just an Euphorian and his human pet, like many others.

Every now and then, another owner and pet will walk past us. At a distance they begin to bring their pets over in the eagerness to show them off to another owner. The second they see that it is Jen and I, they veer off to another path if they can. The scene at the council has caused a scandal, and the repercussions are rippling out through society.

My brothers and I are becoming social pariahs, just as Wrathelder intends. We are in his territory right now, walking freely, but clearly outside the bounds of good taste and propriety. I enjoy the feeling more than I had imagined.

"Tell me how you escaped prison on your world," I encourage her as we enter one of the garden areas.

She looks up at me with a little smirk on her pretty face.

"Why are you assuming I escaped?"

"Am I wrong?"

"No," she admits with a broader grin. "Honestly, it wasn't a master plan. I seduced a guard. Prisons aren't what they used to be. There's no real law anywhere anyway. Being behind bars on Earth now is just what you get for being in the wrong place at the wrong time. I don't believe in right and wrong anymore. All I believe in is what I can and can't do. And I can do most things."

She's a cocky little thing, but I am glad for it. I never expected a human to make me feel braver, stronger, and more determined, but Kahn is right. Her wildness is rubbing off on me, and I like it.

"Wrathelders are city dwellers," I explain to my pet. "They live in the first arrondissement, the circle of spires located around the innermost pillar of the city. They have always wielded much influence in the city. We are striking at the very heart of their territory."

"Good."

"It is also where I will strike at you. You will be punished today, Jen. It will hurt. It will be humiliating. It will be something you never forget, carried out in public."

. . .

J*en*

His words excite me more than I know I should let on. Every time Ark punishes me, I orgasm harder than I ever did before I left Earth. He's warning me as to what he plans to do to me, but it just feels like foreplay.

We're walking toward that big, dark building. The one that makes me feel like the pit of my stomach is rising and expanding to swallow me whole. I try not to be nervous. Ark has this under control. More importantly, Ark has me under control.

"So when we get into the prison, or just outside it, you want me to act up, cause a huge scene, make a distraction, and then you'll make a public example of me in front of everybody?"

"Exactly," he says. "You will do what you do best, and I will do what I do best."

I smile a little, before pointing at a big blimp-like ship in the distance. "Is that it?"

Ark's face falls into a deadly serious expression. "Yes," he says. "That's Wrathelder's ship."

A*rk*

A very large ship is preparing to depart from a dock in Wrathelder's private region, just a few miles from our current location. It is so large it casts a great shadow over all of us and makes the day somewhat cooler than it had been before.

Even at a distance, the large W on the side is very visible, and even if it were not, the fanfare the Wrathelders are making would demonstrate its origin. My only regret is that we cannot stop that ship from departing. It is the first of the Wrathelder fleet going to capture hundreds, if not thousands of humanity's most violent and reckless specimens.

There are big crowds over by the vessel, celebrating with lights and music. I can feel the telepathic charge of excitement and joy coming from those in attendance. Phenix is throwing himself the party to end all parties, and he is doing it at our expense.

"What's wrong?" Jen is worried by my expression. She has no telepathic powers, but she is very sensitive to energy and body language, when she is not choosing to ignore both.

"The beginning of the end," I say, allowing myself a brief maudlin impulse. Wrathelder will cause problems on Earth, and in Euphoria. A dark age is coming. Of that I am absolutely certain. We have begun to fight back, but we are late to the battle.

"So," she says, changing the subject. "While we make a scene, Kahn's already down there, and he's going to somehow give something explosive, a charge or something to Zain, who will escape? Seems like we're leaving the poor guy to basically arrange his own exit."

"A detonator and a charge are more than Zain needs to get out of there," I reply. "Sometimes I think he is only still in there because he's choosing to humor us. We will go down to the prison, and we will do what we can."

. . .

Jen

I hope today's plan works. I hope the ass-whipping I am about to earn is worth it. It's not long before we reach the place we were going, just outside the entrance to the prison. Arkan gives me a look, just a flicker of a brow, and I unleash my demons without needing any more prompting.

"Fuck you, alien scum!" I curse suddenly, making the locals scatter away from us, and drawing interest from the burly guards outside. "You don't own me. You'll never own me! You're not my real dad, and you never will be!"

I don't know where that last part came from, but I roll with it. Seems like one of those old ancestral phrases that floats around the human psyche long after it's ceased to make sense.

"Settle down, pet," Ark lectures. "Or you will be a very sore little human, I can promise you that."

I feel like there's something slightly stiff about his performance. He's not really that stern. He's playing, and I worry others will be able to tell the same way I can.

So I decide to make it real. He has a hand on my collar. I arch my neck and let my teeth make sharp contact with the inside of his wrist. It's a sensitive area with fewer scales. So that's where I bite him. Hard.

Ark's grip on my neck immediately tightens.

"I told you not to bite me," he snaps.

"I know. I don't care." My defiance is organic and entirely real — as is his discipline.

He makes a show of dragging me off the main path and into what I can only describe as the prison car park. There, in full view of an increasing number of guards, he whips my pants down and starts spanking my bare ass for all the alien world to see. There's nowhere for him to prop his leg up, but that doesn't matter, he just picks me up under his arm, wrapping that strong limb around my waist, and spanks me that way.

I curse him out, kicking and flailing as hot bursts of his palm ignite my flesh. This is a real spanking, and it hurts from the first slap. My wails and cries are very genuine as Ark takes me to task.

"Bad, bad little pet," he lectures, his palm meeting my ass hard and fast. All eyes are on us, on me. Every guard is getting an eyeful of my bare ass and everything between my flailing thighs.

"I told you what would happen if you publicly disobeyed again," he growls. "I told you that your displays in front of the council and my family would lead to you being used like the little animal you are,"

I have no idea what he is talking about, but I have the feeling I am about to find out. There are even more guards now. I can see them emerging from the prison, gawking at my bare ass and my pussy on intermittent display every time I kick my legs.

It's embarrassing. I thought it wouldn't be because we're doing this on purpose, but with dozens of big alien guards damn near forming a complete semi-circle around us, I am starting to feel very small and very on display.

"Want to borrow a lash, brother?" One of the guards calls out to Ark.

"Please," Ark says. "These humans cannot be given enough discipline."

A leather-like lash sails through the air, thrown by an obliging sadist. Ark catches it and wastes no time applying it to my ass, the thick hide whipping my own with swift and stinging strokes.

I hope Kahn is inside the prison, though I haven't seen him. I hope Zain is going to get out today. I hope this plan all works, because my bottom and my pride are equally stinging and it will be a long time, perhaps even an eternity, before I live this down.

The gazes of the guards make me feel so small. I am just one little human, surrounded by huge alien men, all of whom find my punishment a matter of great entertainment.

"Let me go! I'll never obey you!"

I guess I have more rebellion left inside me than I thought. Defiance is my favorite pastime even now that I am being made an example of. There's more than just embarrassment. There's a certain heat, a straight up arousal. Ark handles me like I'm just a troublesome little animal, and as small as I feel, I also feel increasingly hot. I'm getting wet, and judging by the growls and sounds emitting from the guards, I am not the only one who has noticed.

Will Ark be mad? Is my display shameful? Will he punish me even harder?

"You're soaked, pet," he growls in my ear. "If I had known you were so receptive to public punishment I would have made sure to whip your ass in front of others before now." His hand is clasped around my hot rear, his fingertips pressed against and slightly into my pussy.

I let out a small, shameful moan, not knowing how far my alien master will push this display.

"Has she learned her lesson?" Ark asks the crowd.

"No!" they shout. I wonder that there are any guards left in the prison at all by now. This is not a world where prisoners escape, but I'm betting Zain could just walk out the front fucking door right now and nobody would notice, much less care. My hot, naked ass has become the star attraction, more so even than Wrathelder's big ship.

"Play along, pet," he growls in my ear, the deep tone of his voice sending excited shivers to the core of me. I don't know what he has in store for me, but I can feel the electric charge that usually means I am about to get fucking laid. Surely he wouldn't do that out here among the guards?

When they say no, I brace myself for the beating of a lifetime. But that's not what Ark has in mind. Instead of another implement, or more whipping, he pulls out the toy. That toy. The buzzing, instant orgasm, alien fuck toy. I must be wetter than I realized, because he slides it up inside my pussy without any resistance. The anal probe seats itself up against my butt, and the sucking fingers find my clit all at once.

He activates his device and I scream in instant orgasm, coming hard and publicly in the sight of the alien guards. These are great muscular beings who deprive others of freedom, the embodiment of cruel authority. And I am coming hard in front of all of them, captured, spanked, and now fucked by this alien technology.

The world seems suddenly bright, and hot, and..

BOOM!

An explosion rocks the city. The guards scatter. Ark pulls the toy out of my still climaxing pussy and yanks my pants up in one surprisingly smooth motion. He sets me on my feet, keeping a fast hold on my collar to stop me from bolting.

I am shocked that the detonation was so large, and that Zain used it so swiftly. I suppose I shouldn't be surprised. Why would he wait? I wouldn't wait. I'd blow myself right out of that prison as soon as I could.

Then I realize that the explosion did not come from inside the dark spire. It came from above. A shockwave of pressure and light is emanating from the heavens. The first explosion is followed by several more, a rapid-fire set of three distinct bangs. Everybody is looking up now. Across the city, heads are raised on the walking paths, hands up to shield eyes from the brightness of the explosions.

We don't notice the little specks of dark at first, not until they become rapidly larger. A big, blackened chunk of shipwreck lands about thirty feet away from us, hitting the concrete or whatever these skywalks are made of with enough force to instantly send cracks spiderwebbing out from the point of impact. I feel the jolt all the way from my feet, up through my spine, all the way to my skull.

The flaming wreckage of the Wrathelder human transport ship is now raining down in hefty burning chunks. They smash into the spiderweb lanes of the city, severing many of them and damaging others. Euphorians are running for their lives as the carcass of the ship comes down.

There is much screaming and panic. That's because they've never seen a world crumble before. Fortunately for me that has been my entire existence. I've seen buildings come down. I've seen people die en masse. The wreckage of my world does not plummet from the sky, but it leaves mass chaos in its wake.

I can feel the energy shift city wide. Nobody here has ever felt the unrest of a tectonic change like this before. They have not suffered through an abrupt shift in reality as they know it. My entire life has been shift after shift. I was barely fucking surprised to be caught by an alien.

The Euphorians thought peace would last forever. They thought they could do anything to anyone, go to other worlds, take sentient beings and bring them back as amusements and nothing bad would ever happen. They thought they could kill fathers and steal mothers and imprison brothers, and nothing would ever happen.

Now something is happening. Something terrible and destructive, something that will scar the city and its people for the rest of their lifetimes.

Ark curses and picks me up, running for safety. The prison would be closer, but he doesn't want to go there for obvious reasons, instead he is forced to make a break for more open territory. It is completely random as to who is hit by the wreckage, and who is sent plummeting miles to the sunless ground below when the path they are standing on becomes suddenly unmoored.

As much as I relish this chaos, I know it could just as easily take us out. I cling to Ark and close my eyes and hope for whatever passes for the best in this situation.

"BROTHER!"

A familiar shout makes me open my eyes as Kahn sweeps down in a shuttle next to us. I thought he would be in the prison handing the charge off to Zain while we made our scene, but it seems he managed to make it to his shuttle. This is very good news for us. A savior is at hand.

"Get in!" Kahn throws the hatch of the shuttle open.

Ark races toward the shuttle and leaps into it, keeping a close and tight hold of me as we make a getaway among the storm of ship which continues to rain pieces large and small, and now a sad ash which turns the perennially bright skies of Euphoria to a dour gray.

There's silence as Kahn pilots the shuttle out of the danger zone. What was almost impossible to escape safely on foot is much easier to clear in a shuttle. It's a matter of seconds to leave the center of peril, and then only a few more minutes to reach the Voros family home.

Not a fucking word is spoken until Kahn lands and we disembark. There is a shell-shocked vibe among all three of us. We stand and stare. I assume they are talking telepathically.

Something is wrong. Not in the ship exploding way sort of wrong. Something is wrong between the brothers. Ark is keeping me in his lap, holding onto me so tightly, as if he's still afraid of me getting hurt. I am confused and a little scared because I do not know what is going on.

"Kahn..." Ark begins to speak out loud.

"Don't ask a question you don't want the answer to," Kahn says.

"Do I need to ask the question? Or do I already know?"

I wonder what they are saying to one another telepathically. There is probably so much I miss out on when it comes to the conversation between these brothers. What they're saying out loud is cryptic and more than a little nonsensical. There's definitely some drama going down.

"We're going to have to vacate the family home. They're going to assume we were behind..."

"There will never be any evidence. Just as there was never any evidence for what happened to our father."

Kahn speaks with a cool, collected tone that is actually incredibly chilling to hear. I haven't heard probably ninety percent of the conversation, but I didn't need to. I've heard enough. Somehow, Kahn is behind this. He blew up that ship.

Moments later, he confesses as much with a casual shrug.

"I decided not to give Zain the charge. I decided to put it somewhere else."

Ark

Kahn has just killed an entire crew and taken out millions of dollars of technology in a single reckless act. He has obliterated all semblance of civilization in this war. And he has come out hard and entirely in favor of fighting for our family.

I let Jen go for a moment so I can draw Kahn into my arms for a hug of the kind we have not shared in many years.

"I didn't know you had it in you," I say, fighting back tears.

This is what a united front feels like. Yes, he was chaotic and unpredictable and dangerous, and perhaps even committed an atrocity, but it was well overdue. Nobody has feared the house of Voros in years. Now they will. Now they will see what befalls the city when we are crossed.

Perhaps I should be horrified by Kahn's actions. Perhaps I should condemn them as being too extreme. But this is what happens when good men are pushed further than they can bear. Kahn wanted peace. He wanted an easy life. But Phenix could not let him, or us, be.

This is the end of peace in Euphoria. It is the beginning of war.

When I release my brother, I see Jen standing there. Not running. Not hiding. Not trying to escape. Instead she is smiling broadly and proudly.

"What is it, pet?"

Her smile brightens a fraction more with that effervescent, wild human glee.

"I told you I'd fuck your world up."

Printed in Great Britain
by Amazon